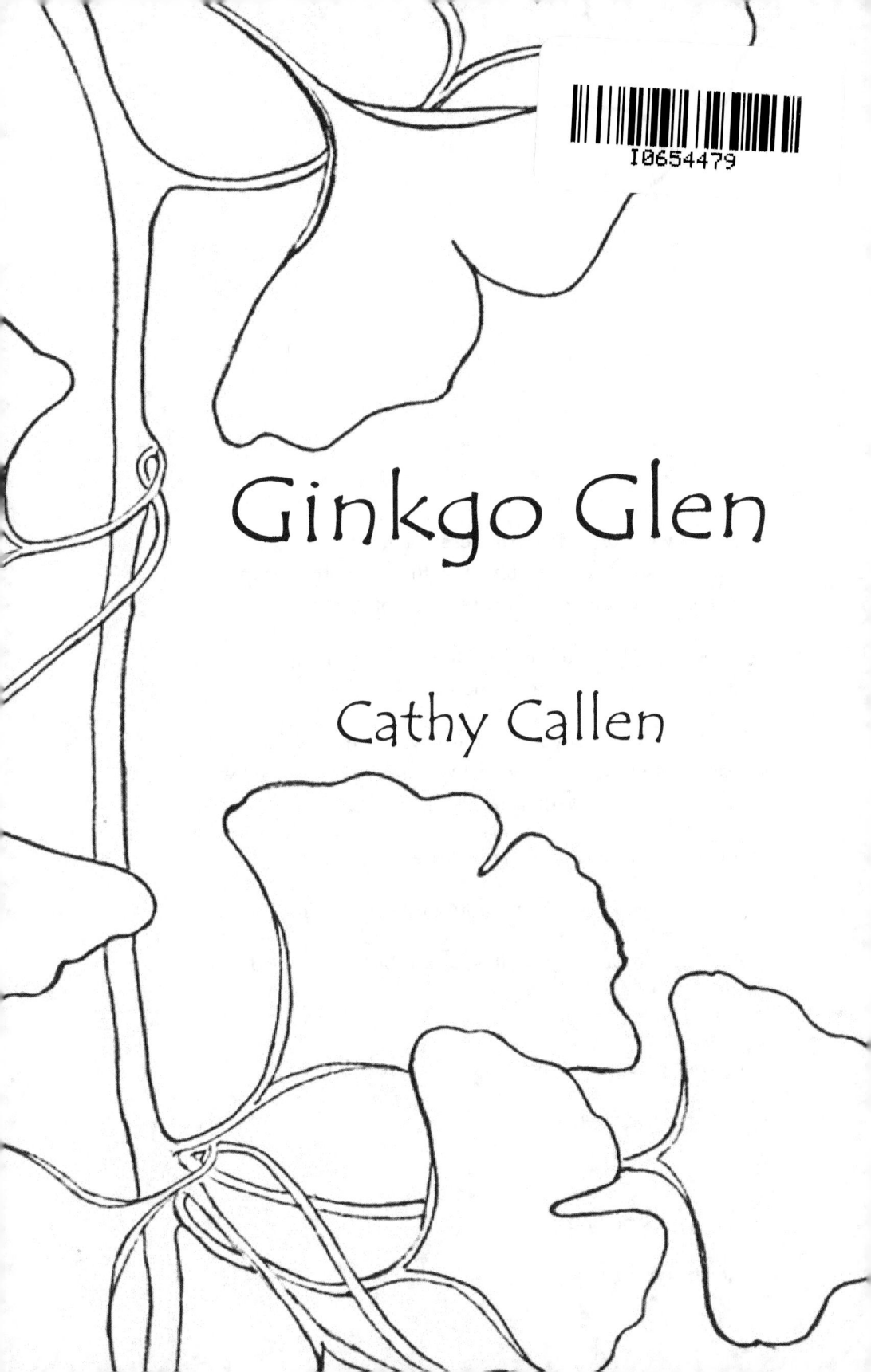

Ginkgo Glen

Cathy Callen

This is a work of fiction. Any resemblance to people living or dead is unintentional. The character Sonia thinks in other people's words. Credits for her thoughts are at the end of the book.

The poem, "The Consent," by Howard Nemerov, is used with the permission of Alexander Nemerov.

The words, "They say life's a journey" are from the song, "It's a pleasure to know you," by Karl Williams, and are used with the permission of Karl Williams.

Front cover watercolor by Janet Rose Bailey

Back cover photograph of the author by Barry Molineux

John Lennon, Dachshund Illustrations by Simon Goodway

ISBN 978-0-9884716-2-7

ISBN-10: 0988471620

Dedicated to my mother

Dorothea Vanderpool Sandford Neff

She had a great laugh!

They say life's a journey, a highway from birth to death

Mapped in despair, and traveled in hopelessness.

Well, they may believe it, but just between you and me

The trick to the travelin' is all in the company.

~Karl Williams

Ginkgo Glen

"What kind of cereal are you having?"

"Cheerios."

"I'm going to boil me an egg. Do you want one?"

"Nah. But you could throw an English muffin in the toaster for me."

"Egad! Look out the window! There's Georgiana! What's that she's wearing?"

"Oh, wow. I haven't seen that get-up yet. Looks like it's one of those HazMat suits."

"What's she doing?"

"I can't tell. Looks like she's scattering little pieces of paper on her lawn."

There was a cluster of homes just inside the western edge of town, built on a small rise of land. The area was called Heavenly Heights because of its slight elevation relative to the rest of the town, and because its developers at the time were nothing if not full of advertising savvy and entrepreneurial optimism. The houses were all three or four-bedroom, had one or two-stories, and were similar in design and construction. The lots on which they were built were also of a similar size, evenly spaced to curve along and around the area's rise in elevation, and were joined by sidewalks and streets, as neighborhoods are. The pièce de résistance for each rooftop was a weathervane shaped like a cloud, with an arrow pointing vaguely toward heaven. All of the homes had been built and sold within a few years of each other, and all were currently owned by their original purchasers. Some neighborhoods have a reputation for being family-friendly and sport dozens of kids who play in the streets and grow up together. Some neighborhoods are transient and are home to legions of temporary residents who come, but mostly go. This neighborhood was defined not by its bland, cohesive appearance, but by its particular collection of residents who had somehow ended up on the same block at one point in time and had grown both older and more like themselves as time had gone by. It provided an ideal stage for the comedy and drama of human life to unfold. Let the curtain rise!

Reuben and Wendy Moreland

Reuben and Wendy Moreland lived on the corner. Reuben lived on the first floor and Wendy lived on the second floor. They had always divided their space this way. Very quickly after their wedding, Reuben and Wendy realized they had different ideas about living space, and so decided that in order for their marriage to work, they would each need space to decorate and own, separate from each other. So, Reuben had taken over the first floor and Wendy had taken over the second floor. They ate all their meals together in Reuben's kitchen, sipping their coffee and reading the daily papers and often observing the comings and goings of their nearby neighbors through the kitchen window. They slept up or down, alone or together, depending on their moods and the weather. The stairway from the first floor to the second floor was like the middle of their marriage sandwich. They tried making love on the steps a couple of times, but it was more than uncomfortable and given up quickly. At least it had been carpeted. The stairway made a more effective communication highway than lovers' nest. They met there often to talk. Wendy would stack things on them near the top for him to retrieve and he would stack things near the bottom for her to retrieve. Interesting newspaper columns, books, notes and cookies were often in transit.

Reuben's given name was Jimmie John. He was embarrassed by his name and always thought it had an uneducated sound to it. He wished his name had been James John, but his mother said they had always planned to call him Jimmie, so why start with James in the first place? Jimmie John had been an OK name when he was a kid. He had a lot of friends who were Billies and Johnnies and Joeys and Timmies, so Jimmie John was just one of the gang. When he got to middle school he tried shortening his name to Jim, but invariably his teachers would take roll and call him by what was on the enrollment form, Jimmie John. In high school, he introduced himself as JJ, or just Jay, for a while, but the kids who had always known him still called him Jimmie John, so just about everyone else did, too. Even though his grades were pretty good, his school counselors seemed to steer him toward vocational coursework. He thought perhaps they didn't take him seriously as a student because of his name. He may have been the one not taking himself seriously, but it was easier to blame someone else. He took his time getting through high school, and finally graduated a year and one semester later than his peers. Jimmie John's slow slog through high school ended in 1983, the same year that the Jimmy John sandwich franchise was launched. Fortunately, it was years before their slogan mocking the slow speed of delivery, became their slogan, or he would have been heckled to death with it. He did make it into a state college, did quite well and eventually graduated, but by this time, he was calling himself Reuben. It seemed like a more sophisticated sandwich.

It seemed inevitable that he would fall in love with a girl named Wendy.

Wendy was short for Windolyn. Her parents told her she had been conceived at a rock concert on a windy day, memorable for a mandolin performer strumming just outside their little camper. She didn't have a middle name. Her parents were wild and crazy when it came to rock concerts, but in reality, they were tidy, practical folks. One child with one name was good enough for them. Wendy's mother had allegedly home-schooled Wendy for the first several years. In reality, Wendy was left pretty much to her own devices, teaching herself to read and write and cut her own hair and fashion things out of mud. When people asked her mother what her child's name was, she would say, "Wendy." If they persisted and asked, "Wendy what?" she would say, "Just Wendy," and so Wendy went through her early life believing her name was 'Just Wendy.' Having only one real name aggravated her no end, and she was grateful to marry Reuben, add his surname to her first and maiden name, and become a normal, three-named person.

Wendy had fallen in love with Reuben in college. She liked his face. She thought it seemed friendly, even when he was not especially intent on projecting friendliness. He had crinkly eyes, and his mouth tended to curve upwards at the outsides. She liked his laugh, too. And, she liked his story about calling himself Reuben. She had been impressed with his field of study, geology, thinking that her family history with rock concerts and his study of rocks was a sign that they were meant to be together. Later, she realized he was studying geography, not geology, but by then the die had been cast, and she already loved him.

Reuben had veered toward a serious academic life once he finally left home. His self-confidence was bolstered by his new name and the new self-image he believed it provided and he was excited to be free and in charge of his own future. The university he attended was quite large, and Reuben was immediately intrigued with the campus maps he received in his orientation folder and also those "You Are Here" location maps placed strategically around campus. They seemed to so easily simplify the complexities of finding classes in old buildings and those under construction, of the roads and bus stops and book stores and the union cafeteria and the dormitories. It wasn't long before he declared geography as his major, with a specific interest in maps. He jumped into his coursework and spent long hours studying his globe, atlases and the state maps he got for free at gas stations. He got a job as a teaching assistant in the geography office and used his meager paychecks to buy an old car. On the weekends, he would take the rural routes out of town and construct his own maps showing where the farmhouses and horse corrals and ponds and interesting stone walls could be found. As he progressed in school, his field of study offered him opportunities to travel, and he took advantage of university-sponsored trips around the country and, once, was able to go on a mapping expedition to northern Greenland. His obvious zest for learning and his ability to pay attention to minute detail made him stand out from his fellow students. He was recommended for and received a prestigious scholarship for post-graduate study, enabling him to pursue and obtain additional degrees.

While Reuben was checking out the lay of the lands, Wendy was having a different college experience altogether. Ensconced on the third floor of White Hall, she immersed herself in the experiential aspects of art. She saw herself not as a deep thinker, but as a deep feeler. Her emotional life, initially expressed in her early mud work, developed into rather bizarre paintings and sculptures as she matured. She participated in several student art exhibitions with such titles as "The Exploration of Nooks and Crannies in Non-traditional Application of Glazes," and, "Identity Crisis Pastels." These were heralded by her bearded and thoughtful professors. Some days she would sit in her corner of the studio and just stare out the window. These reflective moments were often followed by bursts of creative energy and additions to her burgeoning collection of abstract artifacts. She did not seem to connect her college coursework with the idea of future employment.

Reuben was walking on campus one day, headed to teach a class about the geographical features of a tiny group of little-known countries in eastern Europe, when he looked up as he was passing White Hall. He saw Wendy sitting in the window. She was waving madly at him. He looked around, thinking she was waving to someone else, but apparently, she wasn't. She gestured to him to come up the fire escape. He had not done, nor would he ever think he would do, something like this.

But, he did. It was their first staircase. He quickly became enchanted by her carefree, more artistic ways. They began to date, were soon quite attached, and were referred to by their friends as the Sandwich Couple.

Tom and Georgiana Nickerson

Reuben & Wendy Moreland

The house directly across the street from the Morelands was inhabited by Georgiana and Tom Nickerson. Reuben and Wendy had lived across the street from them for over twenty years, but had never actually seen Tom Nickerson. They were very familiar with Georgiana, however, and she was always keen to fill them in on what Tom was supposedly doing while she wandered around outside. Georgiana claimed that Tom worked for the government in some clandestine capacity and that he could only leave the house under the cover of darkness. Wendy had spent many an hour behind the venetian blinds in her second-floor studio, watching for him in the dark, but had never once seen him come or go. Occasionally, Tom Nickerson's mail was mis-delivered to the Morelands, leading the Morelands to conclude that if

Tom got mail, he must exist. Sometimes, Reuben would purposely wait until after dark to take Tom his mail, but it was always Georgiana who answered the door. Once, she even invited Reuben to stay for a cup of tea, which he did. There were lights on in other rooms, but Reuben never heard a sound, and Tom never showed himself. Wendy was sure Reuben had gotten to meet Tom since he was gone so long, and was disappointed to hear that the visit was more about tea than Tom.

Tom Nickerson, as a young man, had been drawn to the fields of biology and chemistry. He did well in high school, taking many advanced placement classes, but his family could not afford to send him to college. He joined the army after high school graduation. He came of age after the Korean War but before the Viet Nam War and completed his tour of duty without seeing combat. He had been a good soldier. He was smart and followed the rules and regulations. He appreciated order and had a knack for keeping track of equipment and supplies, so he spent a good deal of his army career as a supply clerk. His honorable discharge opened the door to continued government employment as a civilian. He was finally able to continue study and work in the fields of biology and chemistry as the military was using scientists to explore the use of chemical weapons. His curiosity about how things worked overrode any anxiety he could have experienced about the use of chemical weapons on people and the environment.

Tom was not a social person, and had not dated in high school or while he was in the army. However, he did pay attention to Georgiana when she came to their laboratory as a church volunteer, bringing casseroles and cakes to this group of scientists who rarely left their laboratory except to sleep, doing important but unnamed work. Tom was kind of a bumbling idiot when it came to interacting with any of these church women, but found it especially difficult making eye contact with Georgiana or engaging in conversation with her beyond comments about her tuna noodle casserole. She was considerably younger than he was, and considerably more attractive, with bright red hair and bright green eyes. She seemed amused by his shyness and seemed to take a measure of delight in making him uncomfortable. Once she realized he liked her tuna casseroles and had a fondness for apple pie, she began a personal crusade of providing these items whenever it was her turn to treat the workers at the laboratory. One of Tom's fellow scientists noticed this awkward interchange week after week, and finally intervened with an offer to Tom to double date with his wife, if Georgiana would consent to go. Though it was excruciating to Tom to ask her for this date, he did. They went to dinner and a movie. She kissed him goodnight. He asked her to marry him over the next tuna casserole. She laughed and accepted.

Sonia and Mark Bittlemeier

Reuben & Wendy
Moreland

Tom & Georgiana
Nickerson

Sonia and Mark Bittlemeier lived across the street and two doors down from the Morelands. Their house was between two sets of neighbors. Sonia called the neighbors on the right the "Commuters," and the neighbors on the left the "Computer Geeks." These neighbors were never at home and in the rare moments when their lives intersected, interaction was brief and inconsequential. The "Marathoners" occupied the house directly across the street, and they, too, led their own lives with little sense of neighborliness. Sonia was glad she had given all these folks monikers, as she had no idea what their real names were. It didn't appear that she had anything in common with any of them except living on the same block for about the same length of time. She did think, however, that "one of these days" she'd make an effort.

Sonia had been a high school teacher. She taught Modern World History and sponsored the school's diversity club. She was married to Mark. He was a landscape architect. Mark had the ladders, mowers, blowers, trimmers, rakes and shovels of his trade, and would have generously loaned them to any of his neighbors if they ever asked, but so far they hadn't. He was a sports fanatic and had a big-screen T.V. Reuben occasionally joined him to watch a basketball game when the university team was playing.

The Bittlemeiers had the nicest yard on the block, with terraces, green grass, layered flower beds and one well-established ginkgo tree. The ginkgo tree was the first landscape decision they had made when they moved into their Heavenly Heights home eighteen years previously. It had been planted at their new home in remembrance of their oldest child, who had died as a toddler. They had had six children altogether, but were now 'empty nesters.' Sonia and Mark were both in their sixties. Sonia was retired, but Mark enjoyed his landscaping business and had no plans to quit.

Sonia had been hit hard by the losses in her life: her first child, the other children growing up and away, her identity as a teacher after she retired. She was often discouraged about her life, disappointed that it no longer provided magic. She wanted everything to be exciting again. She thought she might write up something about her life, something to introduce herself to her children as someone other than their mother, something to leave behind. However, her life seemed too insignificant to her to write about, and she longed to write something of significance.

As she went about her daily routine, different songs, or lines from songs, or passages from books she had read, or phrases she had heard all her life — would pop into her head and take the place of, or prevent her from developing an original thought. She was thinking about capturing those strings of lyrics and clichés and using that collection as her autobiography. After all, that was what was making up most of the thoughts in her head.

Born on a mountaintop in Tennessee . . .

No.

Georgiana occasionally had coffee with Wendy after Reuben left for the university in the morning. Over the years, she revealed few facts about herself, often changing the subject if questions got too personal. She did seem to be aware that she was odd and could probably qualify for a number of psychological diagnoses, not the least of which would have been an obsessive/compulsive disorder. For instance, she told Wendy that, for as long as she could remember, she had been compelled to count things. If she was participating in an exercise class, which she did every Monday, Wednesday and Friday morning, it seemed important to her to know how many other people were participating. She always tried to get an accurate count before they start hopping around, but some folks came late, and some left early. This necessitated counting the class members several times during the hour-long class. She said she could be satisfied to go with the highest number she got at any time during the hour, rather than an average. She said the easiest time to count was when they were marching in place, but counting got complicated when they had to make their arms into windmills or keep track of a ball between their knees. She told Wendy that sometimes she tried to count everyone by looking in the mirrors, but thought that when she did this, she sometimes might count those in the back row more than once by accident. She mentioned that she was pleased that both men and women participated in this class and that she was always trying to count the men and then calculate them as a percentage of the total attendance. She told Wendy that it was rare to have 25% of the class be male, but there was one day in particular that they had a record nine men and nineteen women. She said she could hardly concentrate, trying to do the math, and would find herself continuing one exercise while everyone else had moved on to another one. She could also be sidetracked by trying to see how many class members she knew by name. She could rattle off quite a few in her head, but not all. This was also an exercise in percentages, as she tried to compute how many names she knew compared to how many she didn't. Then, there was a category for those she thought she should know, because she had asked them their names more than once, but now couldn't remember. All of these thoughts kept going through her head as they lunged and kicked and tried to follow their instructor's single, single, double instructions.

Wendy was a good listener. She would cluck, cluck in sympathy, and fetch more coffee. After Georgiana left, she would then spend the rest of her day in her upstairs studio, often staring out the window and waiting for inspiration.

Margaret Sneed

Reuben & Wendy
Moreland

Tom & Georgiana   *Sonia & Mark*
Nickerson   *Bittlemeier*

Margaret was a retired clinical psychologist. Back when she was still working, she had had a private practice, but also was under contract to the local mental health center where she was able to provide services to people without the financial resources to obtain private care. She always had had vivid dreams, often writing about them in her journal and still questioning the effectiveness of the treatments she had provided her patients, long after she no longer worked with them. Her patients were frequent visitors to her dreams and they sometimes posed interesting questions or presented problems she thought she still needed to address for them. Margaret had been married and had two sons. She was now divorced and somewhat estranged from her kids who lived on opposite coasts. Her ex-husband, Bruce, often stopped by to talk politics, fix things around the house or have sex with her. Sometimes Margaret couldn't remember why they divorced. Other times, she couldn't remember why they had married in the first place. Margaret kept pet Sugar Gliders. They reminded her of bats, which seemed fitting for her career.

Margaret bought her house in Heavenly Heights after her clinical practice was solidly established, and long after her divorce from Bruce. The house had four bedrooms on the second floor. It seemed extravagant for a single person, but all the rooms were used for particular purposes, and were therefore necessary in her own mind. She kept one south-facing "bedroom" entirely empty except for a small yoga mat in the center of the room, and used the space for clearing her mind and practicing her own form of meditation. The adjacent south-facing bedroom was for her shoes. She had a lot of shoes. Bruce had built shelves for her along three of the walls, and she kept her shoes in orderly rows. The shelves along one wall were exclusively for athletic shoes. She kept every pair she ever had, partly to remind her of all the exercise she had once done to wear them out. The shelves on a north wall contained boots and slippers and a few pair of leather flats. The remaining shelves were for dress shoes and heels, none of which she wore any more, but they helped to remind her that she didn't have to wear them if she damned well didn't want to. The shoe room had large windows, looking out into her Heavenly Heights neighborhood. This room was also home to a multitude of house plants, most of them thriving due to an abundance of sunshine. The two rooms across the hall were used in more ordinary ways. One was used as a library and reading room. Bruce had also built the shelves for the library room. Margaret had more books than shoes. She had read all of them, sometimes more than once, not on purpose but because she forgot she had read them. She kept a separate shelf just for books she knew she would remember she had read, because they were distinctive and memorable. The rest she alphabetized by author, and noted that many of the authors she liked had names beginning with M. The M authors had several shelves: May, McCall, Michener, Miller, Mina, Moriarty, Morrison. Margaret liked to keep the ones she bought, though she freely loaned books to friends, and welcomed them home to their spots as they were read and returned. There was a comfortable chair and good light in the library room, but Margaret didn't like to read in there. She preferred to read downstairs in the kitchen. The fourth bedroom on the second floor was Margaret's actual bedroom, combined with an office for her computer, her file cabinets, her journals containing her recorded dreams, stacks of magazines and articles clipped from newspapers, a dresser, a closet full of jeans, and a large cage for her three Sugar Gliders. She felt she could use a fifth bedroom.

Sonia loved teaching. She followed the state guidelines for her subject material, but had a lot of leeway in her presentation and focus. While her students gained the required experiences in reading, writing and speaking about world history, its intellectual trends, revolutionary movements, political ideologies, economic theories and geographical impacts, Sonia's emphasis was always geared toward interpersonal dynamics. Not only would her students be exposed to course content, they would be guided to be good listeners, to consider multiple points of view, and to treat each other with respect. She hoped the discussions they had in class would promote kindness and carry over into interactions her students had outside of class. Sonia had always admired those historical and current public figures who took the high road, looking for compromise and seeking peaceful solutions to difficult problems. She made sure her students were exposed to the ideas of world leaders who set good examples by their behavior. Photographs and quotations by Nobel Peace Prize recipients and nominees were posted on the walls of her classroom. Students were assigned these public figures for research, writing, and class discussions. She hoped to influence her students to emulate these leaders and reject violence.

Teaching, though exciting and rewarding, wasn't quite enough for Sonia. She longed to be a mother. She and Mark were married for several years before they realized that a pregnancy would not be forthcoming. They eventually made the decision to adopt a child, and specifically to give a home to a child who might not be easy to place. They went through the adoption preliminaries and were easily approved. Not long after that, they were notified about a six-month old child of Chinese descent, who was available for adoption. She had a serious heart defect and the Bittlemeiers were told she might not live for long. They both felt sympathy for this child and agreed that if her life was to be short, they should give her a home and make her life as full of goodness and love as possible. They decided to name her M Theresa, after Mother Theresa, even though they weren't Catholic. They couldn't really call her "Mother" so they called her Emmie. They hoped that by having this name, Emmie might be provided with a measure of protection against her diagnosis, and perhaps even reverse the dire prediction that had been made.

Sonia and Mark were delighted to be parents and delighted with Emmie. She was a sweet, affectionate child. They credited her with somehow unleashing their fertility, as not long after adopting her, Sonia found out she was pregnant. As she grew larger and larger, it was confirmed that not one, but two babies were on their way. Life at the Bittlemeier house became increasingly complicated.

Sonia and Mark had hoped that with good medical care, Emmie would be able to overcome her heart problems, but this was not the case. She was just three when she died, and the twins Matt and Marty were barely a year old. The activity needed to keep her family moving along helped to dispel the sadness about losing Emmie. Sonia subsequently became pregnant with Bertie, and was pregnant yet again when she signed her family up to participate in the "Hands across America" event in 1986.

May 25 fell on a Sunday that year. It was Memorial Day weekend, and that particular day became memorable for Sonia and Mark for many reasons, not the least of which was because it was the day their newest child, Jimmy, was born. The circumstances surrounding his birth and delivery made his entry into the world impossible to forget. Sonia, Mark, Matt (age 5), Marty (age 5) and Bertie (almost 2), were standing in a line of people that stretched from coast to coast, 4,125 miles long. They were holding hands with strangers who were holding hands with other strangers who were holding hands with other strangers, joined together in a mostly unbroken line of over 5,000,000 people, singing along with the song

"Hands across America" as it blared from car radios near St. Louis, Missouri, when Sonia's water broke. She was not entirely surprised, as she was nine months pregnant, but still, it was problematic. She had been strongly advised (ordered) to stay close to home. Mark had initially refused to consider Sonia's intent to participate in "Hands across America" given her condition. However, Sonia's argument that this was a once-in-a-lifetime event and her apparent resolve to participate alone if he wouldn't go, persuaded him to reluctantly load the family into their station wagon and drive the family to the spots in line that had been assigned to them. Since "Hands across America" didn't go through their state, it was a journey of nearly 300 miles one way for them. They left before sunrise, arrived safely and parked the car in a Safeway parking lot. They then joined the throngs walking several blocks to join the line. The weight of her child in her belly and the frantic pace to reach the line dragging their three younger children set off alarms in Sonia's head, reviving the not too distant memories of other pregnancies and other physical sensations and other babies demanding to be born. Before her water broke and before taking up their assigned spots in line, she had twice visited the Porta-Potty, hoisting herself into the small space, and praying that her child would not drop into this public toilet. She had emerged from the Porta-Potty each time with her child still in place and with renewed resolve. The event was to begin at 2:00 p.m. in their time zone, and her water broke precisely at 2:00 p.m. She stood in her puddle of amniotic fluid, a grimace plastered to her face, for the entire 15 minute event. Sonia did not consider herself a martyr. Instead, she felt that the enthusiasm and energy coursing through joined hands from New York to California, portended a good future for this new child. What a day to be born!

As soon as the event ended, Mark (sporting an "I told you so!" expression) left Sonia leaning against a telephone pole and hastened to retrieve the car, carrying Bertie and dragging the twins. Sonia didn't want to take anything away from this grand, nation-wide experience for the jubilant crowds around her, so she tried to project an aura of just another happy citizen, albeit one standing in a puddle, though surrounded by dry earth. She prayed that Mark would be able to get to the car, find her, and pick her up before their baby had to be delivered by some of the strangers' hands that had crossed America. It was only later that she could appreciate learning that the event had raised millions of dollars for America's poor and homeless, and that her hand–to-hand connections that day had included President Reagan, Yoko Ono, Whoopi Goldberg, Lily Tomlin and at least 54 Elvis impersonators.

The family of five did make it to a local hospital and returned home two days later as a family of six. This brief interlude in the hospital was a restful godsend for Sonia, and an exercise in the true meaning of parenting for Mark as he cared for their older three children in a motel, in the hospital lobby and at several McDonald locations.

One final pregnancy came several years later as a not unwelcome surprise not long after Sonia's 42nd birthday, completing the family with the addition of Baby Del. Having the four boys, with their daughter Bertie in the middle, caused Sonia to constantly reflect on her social studies curriculum in regards to peaceful resolutions to conflict.

As soon as Reuben left for the university, Wendy got dressed. She was keeping an eye on Georgiana out her window. She thought this was going to be a 'coffee with Georgiana' morning for sure. What was the deal with that lime green HazMat suit?

Wendy crossed the street and called out, but Georgiana didn't appear to hear. The outfit she was wearing covered her completely, including her head, and the little plastic-covered opening for her eyes was turned away, so she didn't see Wendy approach either. Wendy gently reached out and touched her arm, causing Georgiana to startle.

"Oh!" she said.

"Georgiana, what are you doing?"

"Actually, I'm trying to count chiggers."

"Hmmm. It seems early in the year for chiggers. How's it going so far?"

"I just got started, so my sum total right at the moment is zero. And, yes, it's early for chiggers, but this can be a baseline."

"How can you possibly count anything wearing that outfit? It doesn't look like you can move very easily."

"That's true. But, at least I won't get bitten today."

"Why don't you come over for a while and we can have coffee and talk. I think I could hear you better if you could pull that hood off, and I don't think you'll get bitten at our kitchen table."

"True. I guess I could take a break."

They crossed over to Wendy's house. Wendy persuaded her to leave the top part of her HazMat suit in the garage. Without the hood, Georgiana's pure white hair fell straight to her waist in a sharp contrast to the green suit covering the rest of her. Her face was weathered and showing some age, and not a few whiskers around her nose and below her chin; Wendy guessed she was nearing 80.

"Where do you get outfits like the one you're wearing?"

"Tom got it for me."

"And, how is Tom today?"

"He had to be out all night, so he's kind of groggy this morning,"

"It seems like he'd be old enough to retire by now. Is he thinking about that?"

"He's still able to do the work, and he has special skills that they need."

"I see. So, counting chiggers. How does a person do that, and, then I'm sorry, but I have to ask, why do you want to do that?"

"Chiggers bite me. I like to know what I'm up against. If I knew how many there were for sure, I could make a plan."

"So, first you count. Then what?"

"OK. I'll tell you what I have in mind. Just don't laugh at me!"

Wendy gave Georgiana a pat on her arm and a reassuring smile.

Georgiana continued, "I've told you before that I like to count things. Chiggers are things that could be counted, and I have a lot in my yard. In fact, just as a rough estimate, I'm guessing there are a gazillion chiggers just in our front lawn. This is clearly an exaggeration, as I'm well aware, but it's a number I like, and I doubt that it is far off."

"So, are you going to go with an educated guess, or will you really be trying to get an accurate count? Who can even count to a gazillion? Is that like a thousand trillions?"

"I think you're making fun of me."

"No, no I'm not. I'm just trying to follow along."

"Well, I know I can't count to a gazillion, but I'm willing to extrapolate if I can get a good representative sample. I chose gazillion because I felt I was up against a formidable enemy, and gazillion seemed like an appropriate estimate. You know, there are lots of blades of grass, and there could be chiggers on every blade of grass. I didn't want to count the blades of grass because they aren't bothering me."

Wendy nodded, fascinated.

"If I could hear," Georgiana continued, "I'd bet the whole lawn would be buzzing with the sounds of those little chigger jaws, opening and closing, practicing their biting techniques and just waiting for me to walk by so they can bite me. My question is, if I do get bitten by one, what do the other gazillion-minus-one chiggers eat? There aren't bunches of other folks walking around my yard for them to bite. It seems like a total miscalculation on God's part to create so many when maybe only one or two ever get to eat. I wonder, too, if I carry one inadvertently into the house and it crawls up my calf and bites me behind my knee and then drops off, what does he do in the carpet for the rest of his life?"

"You make some good points."

"Do you think there's something special in my chemistry that makes them focus on me? If I walk outside, are chiggers making a beeline for me from every direction? Wouldn't this much activity from so many directions make the grass swirl?"

"Well, I do think there's something special about you."

"The best chigger bite prevention method is obviously to stay inside. This isn't always possible, so I have a deterrent procedure to use when I have to go outside."

"What's that?"

"As they say in football, the best offense is a good defense, so here's what I do. In the morning before I go outside, I go into the garage while the garage doors are still closed. I remove my clothes. I have a jar of Vaseline right there on the shelf, and I grab a glob of it and smear it around my ankles, my knees, and my waist. I also put a ring of it around my neck. You would think that a chigger would think twice before heading up my legs once they notice this trap."

"You would think!"

"I did the Vaseline thing this morning, and then, for extra protection, I put this HazMat suit on that Tom got me and then I sprayed myself all over with Avon hairspray. I heard they didn't like that and I've had that hairspray forever and don't use it anymore for my hair. Once I was all greased up, suited up and sprayed up, I opened the garage door and emerged slowly, scanning the driveway for the tiniest of movements. I can't see all that well with the suit on. I won't know until later how well this strategy has worked."

"Hmmmm."

"To be honest, I have never seen a chigger stuck in that stuff. But, I'm not sure I've ever really seen an actual chigger. I'm getting bitten by invisible bugs! I know they're out there and I plan to figure out where they are and how many they are and do something about it!"

"Why don't you just have your yard sprayed with an insecticide?"

"No!" Georgiana looked shocked that Wendy would suggest this. "I mean, no, I can't do that. Tom doesn't believe in spraying chemicals. I have to think of a better way."

"I didn't mean to upset you."

"I'm not upset. Frustrated mostly. About the situation."

"OK, Good. What are all those little papers you were spreading around?"

"Oh. Those are chigger traps."

"Chigger traps."

"Yeah. I took some of that sticky fly paper you can get at the hardware store, cut it into squares and glued them onto bigger squares of white paper. I made 50 of them. Each one is numbered and corresponds to a grid I have inside on graph paper. I put them in the yard, ten rows of five each. Later, I'll be able to pinpoint where the most chiggers reside by counting how many have gotten stuck on each numbered square."

"Very organized."

"When we finish having coffee, I'll go stand in front of one of the papers until some chiggers see me. They'll have to crawl across one of the papers to get to me, and then they'll get stuck. I can just move down the rows, standing in front of each square for a few minutes to get their attention. Tonight, I can collect the squares, study each one, write the total number of captured chiggers on each square of my graph, and I'll know where they like to congregate best. I don't have much of a plan after I get that information. For sure, I'll avoid the congested areas of the grid."

"Well, you've given this a lot of thought, Georgiana."

"Yes. Developing a careful plan gives the best chance for success. I'm hoping the sticky fly paper will do the job. I had to affix it to the white paper because it's sticky on both sides and I didn't want it to stick to the grass and make it difficult to mow."

"Be sure to let me know how things work out."

"OK. But probably not today. I have to implement the plan and see if I need to adjust it at all. Later, I'll definitely curse any little devils who have managed to bypass the Vaseline and the HazMat suit and bitten me. You won't need to hear that! I do worry about what the tons of Vaseline will do to our washing machine."

"Coffee?"

Georgiana was not the only neighbor to have coffee with Wendy. Quite often, Sonia Bittlemeier would stop by, usually to ask advice. She especially sought Wendy's counsel regarding her attempt to write her autobiography using only song lyrics, lines from poems and clichés. Sometimes she'd get stumped, trying to relate one of her life events or emotions to a particular lyric and being unable to think of an appropriate one. She told Wendy, "It seems as though every emotion I could feel has been felt by someone/everyone else, and immortalized in a poem or a story or a song, more succinctly and memorably than anything I could write. *There's nothing new under the sun.* It was new once, and now everything else is a knockoff." Wendy hadn't read what Sonia had assembled so far, but was looking forward to it.

One of Margaret's clients had been a young, thin, nervous type who expressed an interest in overcoming his addiction to smoking. For many weeks, he would come to the clinic, sit across from Margaret, and detail his attempts during the week to abstain from purchasing cigarettes. He was never able to abstain from purchasing them. He then would detail his attempts to avoid opening a pack of cigarettes. He was never able to abstain from opening a pack of cigarettes once he purchased it. He would then detail the drawing out of a cigarette from the pack, the feel of it between his fingers and his lips, the lighting of each one, and the pleasure he felt when he inhaled the smoke. As he sat in her office, he would fidget and tap his pocket repeatedly to assure himself that the cigarettes were still there and that he would be able to have one soon. Margaret recognized the strength of his addiction, and suggested various treatment techniques, all of which he resisted. After making no progress with him over several months, she said to him, "Look. If you want to smoke, smoke. If you don't want to smoke, don't smoke." He seemed quite surprised to hear her say this and was quiet for a moment. Then he thanked her for giving him permission to smoke and said he could use what would have been future clinic fees toward the increasing price of purchasing cigarettes.

Wendy had gone through several creative phases with her art, and had focused on different materials as she moved through these phases. She had painted in college, and had enjoyed sculpting. Her paintings were abstract, often splattered using the Pollack approach to a canvas; several of these pieces still hung in the Moreland house, on the first floor. Reuben said he liked them, hanging them in and among maps of the Outer Hebrides and Cape Town, and setting off his eclectic collection of bean bag chairs, teak bookcases and lamps with stained glass shades from Penney's. Wendy didn't stick with oils or pastels long enough to master essential techniques, and her paintings had never been commercially viable. As for sculpting, she had her heart set on creating famous artists and musicians out of marble. She did make a John Lennon out of wire and paper maché, though this piece would need an identification label in order to be recognized by its viewers. The long hair, wire-rimmed glasses and guitar did help somewhat. This life-sized John greeted visitors to the Moreland home just inside the front door, where he stood dutifully day by day, keeping watch over the family's sets of car keys conveniently hanging from his two fingers, raised in a peace salute. Paper maché John was an "only," like Wendy. She gave up sculpting after creating John, partly because the use of paper maché had been intended as a prelude to working in marble, but she found out that blocks of marble were inordinately expensive. In reality, it was not the expense that caused her to give up sculpting, but the realization that sculpting in marble would have taken so long to do and because she really had no clue how to go about it.

Wendy was interested in ceramics for a while. She seemed unable to manage the symmetry necessary to keep the potter's wheel under her control. Her ceramic pieces often took on the look of a preschooler's thumb bowl or some unidentifiable animal. After her interest in painting, sculpting and ceramics subsided, and with continued encouragement from Reuben and funding from her doting parents, Wendy developed an attraction to the art of weaving. She bought an old loom at a barn sale and taught herself how to set it up. She loved the feel of the yarns and was smitten with all the wonderful colors available. After quite a bit of experimentation, she was able to produce long runners in those wonderful colors she loved. These were usually wider at one end than the other, not by design, but by lack of skill. Wendy continued to make them anyway, folding up one after the other and placing them in a wicker trunk in her studio to think about later. Her easel, potter's wheel, loom, wicker trunk and buckets and cases of supplies nearly filled her small, second floor studio, leaving barely enough room for her comfy chair by the window.

Wendy didn't stick with one form of expression long enough to be considered professional in anything she tried. She always just wanted to already know what she needed to know, and jump right into producing what she imagined. Developing expertise through practice was a skill that eluded her and felt mundane. She had a creative soul but had always been short on follow through. Her artistic tendencies were like little explosions of light that lit her up, but burned out quickly. Her current interest was in constructing art from light, and needing to know how to do it. She had followed the artistic career of Dale Eldred and was thrilled when he illuminated the outside of the state capitol building with rainbows of light. She had been to Las Vegas and New York City and had neon and digital lights flashing in her mind.

Sonia was a bit overweight. She had given birth to five children, including one set of twins, and with each pregnancy she had added not only to her physical girth, but to her anxiety about her size. She thought she probably needed to lose a few pounds, but also needed a new focus for her life. Her heart felt heavy, she thought, because she no longer felt needed.

Getting involved in a project of some sort might chase away the blues. A weight-loss project that could benefit her might help. A weight-loss project that could also benefit others was more motivating to her way of thinking. Even though she felt nothing was new under the sun most of the time, she did have one idea that she thought was original. If implemented, it might help her lose weight and might even be something other people could try.

Sonia's theory was that people were fat, of course because they ate too much, but also because their bodies had already decided what size they wanted to be. People felt the most like themselves at that weight, even though in their minds they believed they wanted not to be fat. The trick, it seemed, would be in fooling the body into thinking it was what it wanted to be, when it no longer was. Could she be less fat if there were a way for the body to think it was fat when it no longer was?

Sonia had read that little children who had difficulty paying attention were comforted with the use of weighted vests and blankets, and wondered if fat people, or a fat person, could lose weight by wearing a vest that had pockets in it for weighted beanbags. Every time the fat person lost one real pound of weight, s/he would put a one-pound weight in the vest s/he was wearing to take the place of the pound s/he had lost. S/he would always wear this vest with its pockets full of weighted beanbags unless s/he was having an outing or wanted to be less fat for an afternoon or evening. When s/he wore it, her/his own weight plus the weights in the vest would always add up to the same amount, but when s/he took off the vest, Voila! S/he would be not quite so fat underneath.

The best of both worlds! "This could be an Ecclesiastes invention," she thought. "*A time to cast away stones, and a time to gather stones together, a time to get and a time to lose, a time to keep and a time to cast away....*" After making an experimental vest for herself, she could make vests for other people wanting to lose/keep 5 lbs., 10 lbs., 15 lbs., etc., with 5, 10, 15 (etc.) pockets and provide the appropriate number of beanbags with each purchase. If she could make something that was useful to others, perhaps her heart wouldn't feel as heavy either. Sonia carried these thoughts in her head, but could never quite dust off the sewing machine to create the vest she was imagining.

"How did the chigger count go, Georgiana?"

"Well, as you know, the wind came up."

Of course, this was painfully obvious, as all 50 of Georgiana's chigger traps had blown away and were now adorning trees and bushes up and down the street like large exotic blossoms, or were stuck by flypaper to the sides of houses and the windshields of cars. They may or may not have had chiggers embedded in them; the total count was unknown. Wendy offered to help retrieve some of these data sheets, but Georgiana just shrugged and said that was OK, she hadn't gotten bitten in her HazMat suit and for now, she'd just count squirrels.

Reuben was attending the State of the Map conference in San Francisco. Wendy went along, as she often did when Reuben traveled. How Wendy would spend her free day in San Francisco was never in question. She would, of course, make an adventure for herself. Perhaps she would visit the San Francisco Museum of Modern Art. Perhaps she would hang out on the Berkeley campus and pretend she was in college again. Perhaps she would cross the Golden Gate Bridge on foot. She was just dreaming about these possibilities when the hotel office delivered its 6:00 a.m. wake-up call. She fumbled for the phone in the dark. Reuben more quickly sprang into action, answered the phone before she knew what was happening, turned on the bedside lamp, kissed her briefly, and jogged to the shower. Always alert, efficient and energetic, he was immediately awake and making his way through his first tasks of the day.

Still somewhat lost in her lingering dream, she brushed the hair out of her face, sighed, slipped her legs over the edge of the bed, and sat. Then she stood, sighed again, and straightened the bed so the maid would not think ill of them. Her energy depleted, she sat then upon the neatened bed and listened to the sounds of her husband in the shower. She knew he would scrub well, washing every part and piece of himself carefully, perhaps using a whole bar of hotel soap as he made his way from head to toe: once, twice, three times. She could hear him set the shampoo bottle on the edge of the shower, imagined him lathering his curly gray head of hair, rinsing and repeating, just like it said in the directions. She heard the water turn off and the towel slide off the rack on the back of the door and knew he would dry himself vigorously until all of his skin was dry and polished and as alert as he was. His hair required much attention or it reverted to an unruly state. Dry it. Dry it. Dry it some more, and then he would brush it, forward, backward, sideways, repeatedly until the lovely tangled curls were lined up, managed, and as flat as possible. She had watched him shower, dry off, and brush his hair hundreds of times, more in the earlier stages of their marriage when she might have been part of the soaping, scrubbing, shampooing, rinsing and toweling dry, but doubted that such a distraction had ever occurred on the morning of a national conference. She could hear him plug in his shaver. She had watched him shave many times, too. He was one of the few clean-shaven men she knew any more. He would twist and pull his face with his free hand, ferreting out the nubs of hair that had tried to grow overnight, until they disappeared. Finally, his clean face, clean hair, and clean body would emerge from the bathroom, clothed in a pair of clean white jockey shorts.

He seemed happier at this moment than at most other times of the day, hair conquered, dirt and grime conquered. He seemed jubilant, fresh, happy. She loved the way he looked when he emerged from the bathroom. She would be sitting there on the edge of the bed, listening and waiting, and when he came out, he would come to her, smile, grab her cheek or chin, kiss her swiftly and then get on with his second favorite part of the day: dressing.

He was a meticulous dresser. She tried to be, but she just wasn't. He pulled his soft white t-shirt carefully over his groomed hair and face, and tucked it into his underwear. Clean socks, probably new. Wool. High quality. Slacks that never looked worn. He was a minimal impact clothing-user. She would watch him iron his shirt, put it on, fold it in back to fit well into his slacks, zip up the front. The belt through the loops, the tie, the button-down collar. Eventually, when it seemed as though he knew everything was perfect yet again, he might notice her, and smile. He knew he was handsome. He knew he looked great. She was sure he liked having her watch him.

At this point, he might shine his shoes again, or re-brush his hair, but then he would leave to get her some coffee while she gazed at the mound of soft pillows. She tried without success to reconstruct her dream and think about what she was supposed to be doing. She was aware that he had gotten all the genes for self-care and that she hadn't gotten any. He cared how he looked. She did too, sort of, but not really. She did, though, try to please him. There was an unwritten contract between them, that when she met him and his colleagues later in the day, she would also be clean, attractive, and wearing an outfit well-chosen for whatever lay ahead. She never really knew what this was, but tried earnestly to anticipate the complexities of social occasions and to not embarrass her husband.

He would return with her coffee. They would arrange a time and place to meet, and then he would be off to enjoy his third most favorite part of any day: taking notes. She knew that in ten years, he would be able to find these notes and remember the name of the speaker.

She opened the blinds, calculated her directions by the slant of the sunlight, and reached for her sneakers.

The Marathoners, Stan and Mike

Reuben & Wendy
Moreland

Margaret
Sneed

Tom & Georgiana
Nickerson

Sonia & Mark
Bittlemeier

Stan and Mike lived to run. They were out at or before daylight on the coldest days of the year, the hottest days of the year, the rainiest days of the year and all the days in -between, running a loop through their neighborhood and beyond, day after day, mile after mile, one pair of shoes after another. When they weren't running on ordinary days, they were running on extraordinary days, joining with other athletes as they prepared to participate in marathons. The two of them had enthusiastically committed themselves to a goal of running a marathon in each of the 50 states, as many avid runners do. They ran more frequent marathons close to home, but their out-of-state participation was tempered by time and money. Still, they had managed to collect at least two states a year, and in their best year, they had run a marathon in seven states. They had always run in the same races, and had both now collected 46 states. The only states left for them to run were Hawaii, Alaska, Idaho and New Hampshire. They had run a marathon in Massachusetts, but not the Boston Marathon, even though their running time for their age bracket qualified them to enter. They preferred to think of that race as if it were a trophy on a pedestal, shiny and waiting for the right time to be claimed.

Stan and Mike had both been runners at the same high school, had track scholarships to the same college, and continued to run even as they got older and competed against enthusiasts in increasingly older age brackets. They had purchased their home in Heavenly Heights together as they embarked on their college careers, thinking their combined contributions to a mortgage would be less than they might pay for rent or for dormitory life. They were of a much younger generation than the neighbors nearby. They did not know their neighbors, had little opportunity to engage with them, and didn't care. Stan worked as a writer for a track and field magazine and Mike was involved in the design and marketing of athletic apparel. They both had reasonable incomes from their day jobs, with this income occasionally supplemented by sponsors eager to have their names associated with these talented runners.

Before Wendy met Reuben, she had been involved with someone else, a man she was crazy about and had thought was perfect. It was an intense affair, made compelling by the very nature of first love, by the demands of class schedules and the restrictions imposed on their time, and by the impending separations that summer would bring. Walks on campus, discussions with other students, quick lunches in the Union, drinking wine and studying together were all exhilarating, and made that spring in Wendy's life a time to remember. She existed in a state of heightened personal awareness that seemed especially vivid, set as it was against the civil unrest so evident at that time in the country's history.

As time and circumstances changed, these two went their separate ways. Unbeknownst to him, however, Wendy was left in a bit of a predicament: a pregnancy during her sophomore year of college. Wendy's parents were cool about the situation, and offered to take care of the child while Wendy finished school. However, she made the wrenching decision to give this child up for adoption. She watched the girl grow up in her dreams and marked her birthday as the years went by. She wondered if the girl looked like her, or more like her father. Did she ever have the chicken pox? Was she interested in art? Did she always have a sense of something missing in her life? Was she happy?

By the time Wendy met and married Reuben, she wasn't as sad anymore. She never had another child. Like her parents, one child was enough.

Besides Georgiana and Sonia, other female Heavenly Heights neighbors made their way from time to time down to Wendy's for coffee and conversation. Wendy knew she was consuming way too much coffee and should switch her offerings to de-caf, but the frequent trips to the bathroom necessitated by the caffeinated beverage provided her with much-needed breaks in these conversations, so she continued to serve it black and strong.

Only rarely did Wendy head out to someone else's place, looking for someone to listen to her, or to have a two-way conversation with an intelligent adult. Not that Reuben wasn't a good listener, or wasn't intelligent. It was just different talking with another woman, and Margaret Sneed had become her confidante. Margaret lived three doors down on the same side of the street. She had lived in the neighborhood nearly as long as Wendy, and they had met when they were out taking walks. Margaret was a psychologist, now retired, an entity any neighborhood could use. Margaret spent most of her time thinking about her dreams and looking for meaning in them. She could easily become distracted by them, and was always glad when Wendy stopped by so she could shift the focus to someone else, as she had learned so well to do.

One morning, Wendy confided in Margaret about her lost things.

"It is so frustrating to lose things," she said.

Margaret nodded.

"I mean, I know that the things I've lost are somewhere, but I can't find them, even though I've sometimes looked and looked. Have you lost things that bother you?"

"Well, sometimes I feel as though I've lost my mind," Margaret joked. "I know I can't remember things that used to be important, but as for missing certain items I may have lost, I don't think I've been bothered by that. Is there some lost thing in particular that's on your mind today, Wendy?"

"Well, there are only a few things altogether that I've lost that break my heart."

"You've kept a list?"

"Not a paper list. A heart list."

"Well, tell me then about your heart list."

"These aren't necessarily in order of importance, because all of them are important to me for one reason or another."

"Uh-huh." Margaret fixed her alert blue eyes on Wendy's face.

"One is a little piece of gold that I discovered myself when Reuben and I panned for gold on our honeymoon. The piece was in the shape of a footprint. I have no idea where it is, but I think of it often. I meant to take care of it. It's not the kind of thing anyone would take and it isn't the kind of thing I'd throw away, so where is it?"

"I'm sure that is frustrating for you, and I know you've looked everywhere."

"Yes."

"Go on."

"OK. The next thing I think about is this silver necklace. A girl in one of my art classes in college made it. I used to wear it every day. It was just the right size, kind of abstract silver loops strung together, simple. I remembered having it on when I left home one day, and when I got home, I didn't have it on. I retraced my steps many times, but I never found it. I still look at women's necks when I'm out, to see if they are maybe wearing my necklace. So far, no luck. It just disappeared. I'm no longer in contact with the classmate who made it, and it feels as though I've thrown her away with the necklace."

"I'm sure it does feel that way. Anything else that you've lost that you want to tell me about?"

"Well, there was a child . . ."

"You lost a child?"

"I didn't exactly lose her. I had a baby when I was nineteen, but I gave her up so she could have a good life and I could finish college. I have always regretted it."

"Regretted having a child, or regretted giving her up."

"Both, I suppose. I just can't seem to get past it, even though it was over 30 years ago."

"Do you know anything about what happened to her? Where she might be? Do you want to be found?"

"I am curious about who she turned out to be, whether she has had a good life, whether she knows she's adopted and wonders why she was given up, what she looks like. Sometimes I think I should let her father know she exists."

"You never told him?"

"No. He had a different life in mind. I didn't want him to resent the child, or me."

"Does Reuben know?"

"Yes, of course. I think he's glad in some way that I got the baby thing over with so it wouldn't need to happen again. He was never interested in being a parent. He does think I should register somewhere in case the girl, I call her Grace, would want to find me, but I haven't done that. I have houseplants and cats and other living things that need me. But, there's still a hole in my heart. You had kids, though, right?"

"Yeah, two boys. They live as far away from me as possible and still live in the same country. One is in Oregon, the other in Maine."

"I know you still see your ex-husband—or at least I think I see his car in your driveway sometimes."

"Bruce. Yeah. I can't remember why we were in such a hurry to get divorced. We talk about the boys. He fixes things for me. And, sometimes we still have sex! Then, he goes home and I have my life back."

"Do you miss having your kids around?"

"Actually, I don't. They seemed like a good idea at the time. That was back when Bruce played the guitar and sang to me and it all seemed so romantic: a guitar-playing husband with a yen to sail a boat around the world, two sweet little babies, and me wanting a career and believing that I could have it all. When I realized that the kids needed food and clothes and school and rides and sports, I was overwhelmed. I felt my own sense of myself shrinking to the point that it practically disappeared. It didn't seem romantic anymore and it wasn't fun. Reality hit hard. We split. Interestingly, he wanted the boys and I didn't fight it. He turned out to do a pretty good job with them. I think I was born to be selfish. I just wanted to be left alone."

"So, life is good now?"

"Pretty much."

Susan Cochran

Reuben & Wendy
Moreland

The
Marathoners

Margaret
Sneed

Tom & Georgiana
Nickerson

Sonia & Mark
Bittlemeier

Susan lived next door to Reuben and Wendy. She bought her house shortly after they did. She seemed to have a lot of money, sources unknown. She raised miniature dachshund show dogs, and wasn't very friendly. Her dogs were yippy little things who snapped as if to bite when anyone but Susan attempted to get close to them. Susan's back yard was enclosed with a chain-link fence and was the only house on the block to have a fence. The covenant that governed the Heavenly Heights subdivision expressly forbade fences. However, Susan had installed one anyway. Inside the fence, the yard was cluttered with various dog paraphernalia, bins, bowls and trash. Though there was often a light in an upstairs window, there was only a rare sighting of her. Wendy thought Susan might have as many as six dogs, but since they all looked and acted about the same, she wasn't sure. The few times that Wendy had tried to encourage a friendship, these overtures were rebuffed, often with the excuse that she was "on the circuit," and therefore couldn't be bothered. Sometimes, though, especially in the spring and fall when the windows happened to be open, soft music made its way from the inside out.

"How is your autobiography coming along, Sonia?"

"Not very well, but thanks for asking. I can't decide if the sentences I'm stringing together should tell about the main parts of my life in chronological order—you know, birth, childhood, adulthood, occupation, death, or if I should go with major topics, like love and loss and hobbies, or things I believe in."

"Couldn't you do both?"

"I could, but there are just so many topics to choose from! Emotions, and fruits and clothing and religion. And, it seems as if each topic that comes to my mind has so many songs and poems with good lines and plain old clichés that it's hard to pick."

"There are lots of good clichés about fruits?"

"Well, that's just an example."

"What have you actually written so far?"

"I started with the chronology idea, but got hung up on being born. I thought of *there's a fool born every minute*, and that resonated with me. I might use that. I suppose, if this is meant to introduce me to my kids, I ought to just stick to facts: who, what, when, why, how. Then the script would be as boring as my life seems to have been--in retrospect, at least. They grew up with me, though, and are aware of my tendency to think in other people's words. Seems like it would be more honest, and more fun to write it that way."

Wendy and Sonia were seated at Reuben's kitchen table. It was a beautiful spring day, and the leaves were just beginning to come out on the bushes outside the window. There was a clear view across the lawn and street to Georgiana's house, and in fact, to Georgiana, who was walking around her Sycamore trees and making notations on a clipboard. She had on a broad straw hat, a camouflage jacket and boots, and seemed startled from time to time when something happened in the trees above her that she wasn't quick enough to observe.

"She's an interesting neighbor," said Sonia.

"Yes, she is."

"*A few cards short of a full deck*, though, I'd say. Did you know she's a counter?"

"I did. Has she talked to you about it, too, then?"

"More than once. I guess I don't keep track of things as well as she does."

They both laughed softly, watching Georgiana, not without affection.

Wendy said, "She told me she was trying to get an accurate count of the squirrels in our city."

"Oh, dear."

"She said she knew it was a finite number even though we didn't know what that number was. She said she was spending a lot of time devising ways this population could be counted, knowing it isn't infinite, just difficult to calculate. She said it had really been bothering her."

"She's *a few bricks short of a load*, isn't she?"

"Sonia, honestly. You need to get this autobiography out of your head so that you can have normal conversations!"

"I'm sorry. I guess I just throw in the first thing that comes to mind when I'm talking."

"It's OK. I think we can all be too much ourselves at times. As for Georgiana, she is really into this squirrel thing now that the chigger count proved to be a disaster. She said she wondered what methods would need to be employed to get an accurate number of squirrels inside the city limits at one point in time. It had to be accurate, or what good would it be?"

"God love her. What good would it be anyway?"

"Exactly. It would be a number, and people might say, 'Wow, that's a lot of squirrels,' and then go on about their business. It seems more important to Georgiana than that. She said that even the exact number of people within the city limits at one point in time would be almost impossible to determine. Everyone would have to hold still, and who would agree to that? How long would it take? And then, the squirrels. How many are running in and out of the city's borders at any given time? The time of year for such a count would be important to her, as in, is it squirrel suicide season? In spring and fall they seem to be oblivious to cars, either because they are chasing a potential mate, running away from a potential mate, or in a frenzy because all the acorns are falling and there is so much to do they can't pay attention to cars. How many are flattened by cars just before the count, or fall off of electrical lines or telephone wires (are there still telephone wires for them to fall off of?). She just went on and on!"

"Her light's on, but no one's home."

"Sonia!"

The Commuters

Reuben & Wendy Moreland   *Susan Cochran*   *The Marathoners*   *Margaret Sneed*

Tom & Georgiana Nickerson   *Sonia & Mark Bittlemeier*

They went somewhere every day and came back from somewhere every day—at least there were no cars in the driveway during the day, and two cars in the driveway at night. One car was a fairly classy black SUV, and the other was a not-so-classy foreign car of some type, perhaps a Toyota.

The Computer Geeks

Reuben & Wendy Moreland   *Susan Cochran*   *The Marathoners*   *Margaret Sneed*

Tom & Georgiana Nickerson   *Sonia & Mark Bittlemeier*   *The Commuters*

The windows in their house flickered in shades of blue at night. They could sometimes be seen emerging, pale and squinty in the morning, carrying stuff to their car, and driving away.

Wendy didn't believe in organized religion. She didn't believe in disorganized religion either. Religion just wasn't on her radar. However, she had a healthy respect for Reuben's involvement in his own church. He attended faithfully, and spent much time doing various kinds of volunteer work there. Wendy had met quite a few of his friends from church, admired them even, and supported the various events they held to raise money for worthwhile activities. She enjoyed baking for their annual Bake Sale because it gave her an excuse to make a chocolate cake.

"Sign me up to take a cake to the Bazaar, OK?"

"That's very sweet of you. Yes, I'll sign you up. I think it needs to be at the church on Thursday, by 10:00 a.m."

"OK. I can do that."

Wendy checked to see that she had all the ingredients she needed. Wednesday, after supper, she began assembling the batter. The cake recipe she was using had been in the family for several generations. It was an unusual recipe, in that the leavening was stirred into boiling water and was added last, after everything else was mixed. She followed the recipe, poured the batter into a Bundt pan, and put the cake-to-be into the oven at 350° for 50 minutes. When she checked on the cake's progress after 45 minutes, she noticed that not only had it not risen, it now appeared to be about half the size it had been when she first put it in the oven. She gave it the benefit of the doubt, and let it cook the last five allotted minutes, but when she removed it from the oven, it was clear that she had a disaster on her hands. She knew she could never present it to Reuben's church to be put up for sale. She might not believe in God in the same way Reuben did, but she did believe in a good chocolate cake. As late as it was, she'd just have to make another one. Reuben sympathized with her, and did his part by making a night run to the grocery store to get a new supply of butter, sugar and chocolate squares. While he was gone, she tried to figure out her mistake on Cake #1. She had made mistakes with this recipe in the past, mainly using baking soda that had expired long ago. Back then, she had still been using the first box she had ever bought, possibly as long ago as thirty years. She didn't have much occasion to use baking soda. "There was still some in the box, and I hated to waste it," she had said when that cake didn't rise. She subsequently bought new baking soda each time she made this cake. It said right on the box to discard the remainder one month after opening it, but she had never noticed this. Such a waste. She had checked the date on her baking soda as she had assembled her ingredients for Cake #1, and had, once again, purchased new baking soda, so it wasn't the age of the baking soda that was the problem this time. She walked through the assembly process in her mind. When she got to the last step, adding baking soda to the boiling water, there was no memory of having done this. She had apparently gone to the trouble of buying new baking soda and then hadn't used it at all. Ugh. How stupid. What a waste! Reuben came home with the new ingredients, and with less enthusiasm than she had displayed earlier, she began the task of baking another chocolate cake. It was quite late when Cake #2 came out of the oven.

Thankfully, it was nicely rounded and could pass as a worthy donation to the Bake Sale. Early the next morning, she frosted it, put it into a cake container and labeled it. Then, Reuben drove her down to the church while she balanced the lovely cake on her lap. The two of them walked up to the church, proudly carrying their hard-won cake for the Bake Sale. The doors were locked! They could see people inside, and gestured to one of them to open the door, holding up the cake as evidence that they needed to be admitted, even though the sale wasn't yet open for business. Soon, the door opened a crack. Two hands reached out and snatched the cake before closing the door once again and locking them out. Her hands suddenly empty, Wendy thrust them in her pockets.

"Well," she said. "That was anti-climactic."

"Yes, it was," replied Reuben. "There should at least have been a priest there to bless the cake."

Wendy laughed.

"I mean, they bless the animals. They could at least bless a cake."

She slipped her hand into his and they walked to the car. She loved that man, plain and simple.

Georgiana emptied the lint drawer in the dryer. She had washed and dried her sheets on a Saturday, as she did each week. And, she took the dryer lint and put it into a plastic bag where she kept all of the dryer lint produced from drying her sheets. She wondered how many washings and dryings a set of sheets could endure before disappearing altogether. Therefore, she resisted buying new sheets, and had used the same sheets weekly forever. So far, the sheets still resembled sheets. She also wondered if the lint they produced could somehow be woven into a new set of sheets when this set eventually disappeared. So far, she hadn't needed to worry about this.

"What do you think about Georgiana, Margaret? You're a psychologist."

"Is she that woman who lives across the street from you?"

"You mean you don't know her, after all these years?"

"I haven't really done much with the neighbors, you know? I hang out with staff from the clinic and some of the people who had offices in the same building where I had my private practice. And Bruce. But, I don't know Georgiana. Why are you asking about her?"

"Well. She's just odd. She must be nearly 80 years old. She doesn't seem to go anywhere or have any friends. And she counts chiggers."

"Now you don't hear that every day!"

"No, really. She seems obsessed with counting things. I think she's just lonely."

"Does she live alone?"

"She supposedly has a husband, but we've never met him. She comes over for coffee once in a while, but all she ever talks about is counting things."

"Well, I've seen her out in her yard from time to time, but I've never talked to her. If she's really around 80 years old, she is probably who she is and has gotten used to herself by now. I'm sure she's harmless."

"You've lived here all these years and you've never talked to her? Do you know any of the neighbors?"

"I really don't. I talk to the kids across the street sometimes."

"Kids?"

"You know, that couple that lives in the gray house. They're younger than most of us. They commute."

"Do you know Sonia and Mark?"

"They have the pretty yard, right? I see him out there all the time. Didn't they have a bunch of kids?"

"Yeah. Six! And, she was a teacher! She's trying to write a book, or at least some kind of document to leave for her kids."

"I guess I've just been wrapped up in myself. I don't know any of my neighbors."

"Maybe we should have a block party sometime," Wendy suggested.

Margaret's private practice had tended to draw affluent clients who were experiencing guilt issues: errant husbands, errant wives, young women involved with errant husbands, young men involved with errant wives.

I want to do it, but I haven't yet.

Should I do it?

Would it be wrong if I did it?

I did do it.

Should I tell my spouse, or shouldn't I?

I don't think s/he would find out.

I don't think anyone will get hurt.

I really don't think s/he would mind, but I don't want to ask.

If I did ask, and s/he said s/he would in fact mind, then what should I do, because I really want to do it.

Margaret would ask them why they were struggling with these questions. Could their conscience be at work? Could they perhaps listen to what their own conscience was telling them? Their responses always began with, "Yeah, but . . ."

The doorbell rang.

The young woman on the porch was immediately recognizable. It was Wendy's daughter.

"Hello."

"Hello."

"Would you like to come in?"

"I would."

The young woman entered. She smiled when she saw John Lennon by the door. Wendy invited her to hang her purse around his neck and follow her into the living room.

"So. Here we are."

"Yes. That's true. Here we are."

"How did you find me?"

"It wasn't hard. I was old enough to get a copy of my original birth certificate several years ago, so I've known your name for a while. And, I live here in this town. I saw you at the grocery store last week and followed you around. I was pretty sure it was you."

"What did I buy?"

"Some grapes."

"Oh, yes, I remember. They were Thompson Seedless. On sale."

Wendy and Grace were in Reuben's living room, sitting on Reuben's sofa, staring at each other.

"You have a nice house," Grace ventured.

"Thank you. I live here with Reuben."

"Is he my Dad?"

"No."

"Who is my Dad?"

"Why do you want to know?"

"I just do."

"I'm not going to tell you."

"Do I have any brothers or sisters? I mean, did you have other kids besides me?"

"No."

"Why did you give me away?"

"I wanted you to have a good life with two parents. Did you?"

"My folks are good."

"Did you go to college?"

"I'll tell you about me if you'll tell me who my father is."

"Hmmm. A smart one. I thought you might be."

"My father was smart?"

"Very."

"In what way?"

"In every way but love."

"He didn't love you?"

"I think he did, but it was a big world out there and he wasn't ready to stop exploring."

"What did he want to explore?"

"Everything."

"So you had me, and gave me away, and then you just went on with your life like nothing ever happened?"

"I had you and that part of me died when I gave you away. Then I met Reuben."

"So, you've been married to him for a long time?"

"Yes, for 28 years. You would like Reuben. Do you want to meet him?"

"I guess so. Is he here?"

"Yes, he's back there in his office."

"What's he doing?"

"I never know exactly, but if I call him, he'll come."

"OK."

"Wendy, wake up. You're talking in your sleep again."

"No, I'm not. I'm talking to Grace."

"Again?"

Sonia carried the load of clean sheets from the drier in the basement, upstairs to their bedroom on the second floor and emptied it onto the bed. She pulled the fitted bottom sheet out and piled the rest of the clean laundry on the armchair by the window. As she wrestled with the sheet, trying to figure out which was the top or bottom and which were the sides, she smiled to herself and started humming an old John Denver song, one she always thought of when she was changing the sheets. She tried to remember the words—something about having fun and not getting much sleep and there being a piggy? Was that right? and some hound dogs? Then, as if on cue as she was attempting to string some words and notes together about hound dogs, her singing was interrupted by what sounded like a real hound dog, barking outside, below the window. There weren't many dogs in the neighborhood, and she wondered briefly if it was a stray, or if she was just imagining things. She got the sheet over the four corners of the mattress with great effort and turned her attention to the top sheet. The barking persisted. She walked over to the window to look out. She didn't see a dog, so resumed her task and flapped the flat sheet over the bed, pulling it even at the top and tucking it in at the bottom. The barking continued. This time when she went to the window, she looked out and down. There was a little brown dachshund standing beneath the window barking its fool head off.

"What's the matter, Lassie? Is Timmy in the well?" she said aloud, smiling and shaking her head. Sonia hadn't thought of that line for years, not until a little dachshund appeared distraught below her window. She tried to ignore the barking, but shortly realized how unusual it

was for a dog of any kind to be barking at her house. She did know that her neighbor Susan had several of these dogs, and wondered if it had gotten out without her knowing it. She left the bed partway made and went downstairs and outside. The little dog trotted over to her, looked up, and then started off in the direction of Susan's house. Sonia watched it go, assuming it would now go bark at Susan's door and be let back inside. However, once the dog crossed the street, looked back and realized that Sonia was not coming too, it barked again. Sonia crossed the street and followed the dog to the front door. She had never been in Susan's house, or even on her property. The door was shut, so she knocked. No one answered. There was a doorbell, so she rang the doorbell and waited. There was no response. She tried to look through the little window in the door, and then stepped over behind the bushes to peek in the front window. She couldn't see anything. The dog was now sitting on its haunches and watching her with apprehension. As no one came to the door, Sonia started to walk away, but the dog started barking again.

"What?"

The dog trotted around the side of the house. Sonia didn't like the idea of trespassing, and she imagined that Susan would not like her snooping around. But, then, there was Lassie, leading her around the side of the house, and Timmy might in fact be in the well, so she followed the dog. There were no doors on that side of the house, so she walked back around the front of the house and the garage to the other side. There was a side door to the garage, but it was on the other side of a fence. It had a pet door, obviously to let the dogs go outside but still be contained in the fenced yard. The gate to the fence was not latched, and moved easily when Sonia pushed on it. She went through the gate and knocked on that door. There was no response. She briefly considered entering the house through the pet door, and laughed to herself to think of being found there, stuck halfway in and halfway out. The dog, however, ran through the pet door, disappeared briefly, and then ran back out, barking.

"Hmmm . . .," she said out loud. *"Something seems rotten in Denmark."* Since she was already inside the fence, she walked on around to the back of the house. Susan had a wooden deck with sliding glass doors. The drapes inside appeared to be open. Sonia thought, "What the heck? I'm already trespassing," and went up onto the deck to peer through the glass doors into the living area. At first, she saw quite a few pet carriers and it looked like there were dogs inside each one. Those dogs were now barking along with Lassie. Then, Sonia saw Susan, lying on the floor near the sofa. Sonia pounded on the door but the only response she got was more barking. She freaked out, ran back home and called 911.

When the emergency personnel arrived, they had to break into the house to get to Susan. She was unconscious, but was still alive. One of the first responders asked Sonia lots of questions, but Sonia didn't know enough about Susan to answer them. As the medical folks prepared to take Susan to the hospital, they told Sonia they would call someone from animal control to come get the dogs. Sonia thought that was a bad idea, but wasn't sure what a good idea would be at that moment. After a pause, Sonia made a decision and said not to call animal control because she would take the dogs for now.

And what a parade it was! Sonia led the way across the street with one pet carrier containing one barking dog. Two EMTs followed her, each carrying two caged and barking dachshunds in pet carriers. Lassie trotted quietly along behind.

At the age of 60, Tom had found himself seated in the office of a therapist. He was vastly uncomfortable at the situation, but had decided before he went, that he would listen to what the expert said about his depression, and take any advice given, if it seemed reasonable.

"Welcome. How are you today?"

"I'm fine, I guess."

"Can you tell me what brings you to see me today? Your intake sheet mentions that you have been depressed."

"Yes. That's true."

"Is this a new feeling for you, or have you felt this way for quite some time?"

"It's not new."

Tom was not used to having attention drawn to himself, or to answering questions about his feelings. He suddenly felt as though he was going to have a panic attack. The therapist noticed Tom glancing toward the door and saw the effort it took him to remain seated.

"Let's go back a bit. Why don't you tell me something about yourself, your family, your career."

"OK. I'm 60 years old. I was in the military, then worked for the government. I quit my job last year."

"Quit? Or retired?"

"I quit."

"Were you unhappy with the work you were doing?"

Tom shifted in his seat. He didn't answer.

"Tell me about your family."

"I don't have one."

"Parents? Siblings? Wife? Children?"

"No."

"You don't seem inclined to provide many details. Why are you here?"

"Well, I was advised to come by a donkey."

"A donkey."

"It's a long story."

"I hope you'll come back to tell it to me."

"I'm glad you came back."

"I wish I could say the same."

The therapist inclined her head slightly, then said softly, "Why don't you tell me about the donkey."

Tom hung his head and remained still. After a few moments, he looked up and said, "A couple of months ago, I went to a retreat of sorts. It was just a weekend thing, put on by a church I sometimes went to. I thought it might help me take my mind off things. It was out in the country."

"Yes?"

"To be honest, I had been ready to pack it in."

"Why was that?"

"Well, you see, my wife had died and I couldn't get over it. I had felt responsible. I still do."

Tom paused, then went on. "Anyway, that day, I left the meetings at the retreat and went for a walk. It was a cold day, and cloudy. The weather didn't help my mood at all. In fact, the longer I was outside walking, the worse I felt. Somewhere along the way, I noticed a pack of horses on a far hill. There seemed to be five or six of them. They looked so wild and free. I crossed over a ditch and went to the fence to watch them."

Tom paused again, remembering.

"As I watched, I experienced this intense wish to somehow be taken away by them. I had this idea that I would call to them, and if they came close and I could touch them I could somehow be absorbed into them and that maybe then I'd be wild and free too."

"Go on."

"I did call out to them. I never expected them to come. They were a long way away. But I was surprised when first one, then the others, turned in my direction and began to run down the hill, across the field toward me. Maybe they thought I had sugar or a carrot or something."

"Then what happened?"

"I can't really explain it. They all raced down the hill just like the wind and gathered in a group just out of my reach on the other side of the fence. They were snorting and prancing around and watching me as much as I was watching them. I know it sounds strange, but they seemed to understand that I was profoundly sad and needed something from them."

"And . . . ?"

"I started to reach out. It seemed like time stopped for a moment. I felt if I could touch one of them, I would cease to exist. I would evaporate. It was very intense."

Tom paused, and hung his head again. When he lifted it, there were tears in his eyes.

"But you see. I had felt this strange contract was with the horses. When they got so close to me, the one that came forward to let me touch, was not a horse, but a donkey."

Tom's eyes met those of the therapist, as though the conclusion to the episode should have been obvious. It wasn't. He shook his head slowly.

"So, if I had been able to touch one of the horses, I think I would have figured out a way to quit living. I was halfway there already. But, it was the donkey who came close and let me rub its nose. Because it was a donkey, I came here instead."

"Grief can be overwhelming for anyone. Your wife has died fairly recently?"

"Yes."

"You said you felt responsible. How so?"

"I worked with chemicals. Dangerous chemicals. She died of cancer. I think she somehow was exposed to the chemicals and they caused her cancer."

"I'm sure there was a protocol for handling these materials. Are you saying that you weren't following proper protocol?"

"I always followed the rules."

"Was there any evidence that your work was causing unintended illnesses?"

"No."

"Did any of your co-workers' family members develop similar symptoms?"

"No.

"Has there been an investigation into this?"

Tom sat with his shoulders slumped and didn't answer at first.

"You know, it doesn't really matter if there was an investigation or not, or whether I actually caused some type of contamination that made her sick. I believe it, whether it's true or not. I should have been able to protect her. I loved her. I miss her terribly. I wish it had been me instead of her. She was so alive and fit so easily into the world, and I don't."

"OK. Your wife has died. You feel responsible for the illness that led to her death, although you don't know if this is true or not. You have quit your job. You are experiencing many losses. But, you believe you have been given a sign that it may be OK to get help, and here you are, yes?"

"I guess so."

"Sometimes it's helpful to start with gathering information. You seem very thin. How long has it been since you had a physical?"

Tom shrugged. "I have only thought about her being sick. I can't remember the last time I saw a doctor for myself. We had just bought a new house. She was looking forward to moving into it. She never even got to live there. I think I should sell it, but I can't seem to find the energy to do it, so I just don't, day after day. Pay the rent on the old house. Pay the mortgage on the new house. Sleep. Eat. That's about it."

"I'm going to suggest a plan. We can continue to meet and talk. This is a good place to start. I'm also going to recommend that you visit with your primary care physician, get a physical. You might do well with a temporary medication. Would you do that?"

Tom sat with his head down, not looking at her, so she continued.

"It would be good, too, for you to be around people more. For instance, you could consider participating in a discussion group with people having similar issues with grief. I can give you a resource to contact."

She got no response from Tom.

"Exercise might help as well. Is there a gym nearby that you could join? Sometimes they offer classes suitable for older participants. Also, you might think about moving into your new house, starting a new life. What do you think? Could you pick one of these ideas and move forward with it before we meet again?"

Tom finally looked up. "I don't know if I want anything to change. I'm afraid my memory of her will disappear. I still have all of her things. Sometimes, I just open her dresser drawers and hold her nightgowns to my face. Sometimes I stand in the closet and surround myself with her clothing. Lately, I've been sleeping in her track suits."

"I see."

Tom sat there a few more minutes. The therapist handed him a card with a date and time for their next meeting, and asked him to sign permission for contact with his physician. Tom signed the permission and took the card. He never went back.

Sonia put the pet carriers with the yapping pets in the kitchen and called Mark. She told him about Susan and the six dogs, and asked him to stop by somewhere on his way home to pick up some dog food—she didn't know what kind—and some leashes—probably six leashes. Lassie was not in a carrier and sat looking at Sonia expectantly. She figured all the dogs were hungry or had to relieve themselves, or both, but wasn't sure how to accomplish feeding or "walking" the dogs until Mark got home. *She had so many children, she didn't know what to do . . .*

Sonia decided to call Wendy. She asked her to come over to help her with Susan's dogs. Wendy had heard the ambulance and wondered what was going on. She listened as Sonia gave her the details, and then went over right away. It was easy to see the monumental task that Sonia had taken on, what with five pet carriers full of dogs lined up in the kitchen and one extra dog backed into a corner and barking at her. Sonia told Wendy that she was pretty sure this whole arrangement was going to be a bad idea. And, she didn't think Mark would like it either.

"What if we take one dog at a time to Susan's back yard in a carrier, let that dog run around and do its business, bring it back and then take another?" Wendy suggested.

"There's a doggie door into the house. What if the dog runs into the house and we can't get it to come back out?"

"Right. We should put something in front of the doggie door so they can't go inside. Do you have a piece of plywood or a big bucket or something like that we could use?"

"I'm sure there's something in the garage."

Sonia went into the garage. She didn't see any plywood or buckets, but she thought Mark's lawnmower parked in front of the doggie door would do the trick. Wendy went back to her house and got some woolen yarn. They cautiously approached Lassie with a string of it, intending to hook it onto her collar to use as a temporary leash. Lassie barked and snapped when they got close. Sonia had some cranberry-oatmeal cookies on the counter and held one out to Lassie. This did get her attention, and the two women were able to put some yarn through her collar while she was feasting on the cookie. Then, Sonia pushing the lawnmower and Wendy pulling the barking dog, they made their way to Susan's back yard. They went through the gate, latched it, and parked the lawnmower in front of the doggie door. Wendy let go of the leash and Lassie took off. She did "do her business" fairly quickly, but ran back afterwards, hopped on top of the lawnmower and tried to get to the doggie door. Sonia reached for the string of yarn, but Lassie took off across the yard and a great chase ensued. Two older women, one younger dog, around and around. Lassie won. They couldn't catch her, and there were five more just like her across the street. Sonia sighed and went back for the cookies. By the end of the afternoon, they had managed to "walk" all six dogs and had caught all six dogs, returning five of them to the kitchen in their pet carriers, with one left over, dragged by a deteriorating length of woolen yarn. This was accomplished with the remainder of an entire package of cookies and a couple of cold hot dogs.

In order to keep the dogs straight Sonia and Wendy thought they had better give them temporary names. They weren't sure this was even important, but they did it anyway. They giggled as they looked each one over, coming up with Porky, Dolly, Baby, Archie, Queen Mary and, of course, Lassie. They wrote these names on electrical tape and stuck one on each dog's collar and its pet carrier. That was the end of their dog energy for the day. When Mark came home, he found Sonia and Wendy collapsed on the living room sofa. The five dogs in captivity greeted Mark with their irritating chorus. Lassie was chewing on one of Mark's shoes in the hallway.

"I hope Susan makes it," was all Sonia could say.

"You have to go ask Susan what to do with these dogs," Mark said to Sonia as they were getting ready for bed. "We can't keep six dogs! We can't even keep one dog! We don't have a fence! They'll dig up the yard! They'll bring in fleas! They'll bark all day and eat us out of house and home!"

"We could board them at a kennel," Sonia suggested.

"Do you have any idea how much it would cost to board six dogs for even one day, let alone the possibility of weeks?"

"I'm sure she'd pay us back."

"You don't know anything about her, so how do you know she'd pay us back?"

They got into bed. Just as they were settling in, they heard the pitter patter of little feet. Lassie was too short to hop on the bed, but that's clearly what she had in mind as she jumped up and down, scratching at Sonia's side of the bed and whining. She had been tied to a drawer handle in the kitchen with her new leash and had been given a blanket. The leash was still attached to her collar, but obviously was not attached to the drawer. Sonia couldn't look at Mark as she lifted the dog onto the bed. "Please," she said. "It's just for one night, and I'm so tired." Lassie made quick work of finding a comfy spot between them and promptly fell asleep. Neither Sonia nor Mark said a word, and the house fell into an uneasy stillness.

"Houston, we have a problem."

"Let's see, who could this be? I'm guessing by this opening greeting that it's Sonia!" said Wendy into the phone.

"Ha ha. Wendy, I need to go to the hospital to see Susan and ask her what to do about her dogs. Will you go with me?" Sonia asked her on the phone.

"Sure, I'll go. What about the dogs for now?"

Sonia was already tired of the whole situation. "I say, let's take them all over to Susan's back yard and just let them go."

So, that's what they did.

They got to the hospital and asked what room Susan Cochran was in. The volunteer at the information desk looked her up on the computer and told them that she was in intensive care, and gave them directions to that area of the hospital. When they arrived, they asked to see Susan.

"Are you family?" the nurse asked.

"No, we're neighbors."

"I'm sorry. Only family members are allowed to visit patients in intensive care."

"But we have her dogs!" Sonia blurted.

"I'm sorry. I can't let you visit."

"Can we at least find out how she is and how long she'll be here?" Sonia pleaded.

"I'm sorry, no."

They drove home. "We could take them to the Humane Society," Sonia ventured.

"Sonia, these are show dogs! They're probably worth a lot of money. We can't just dump them at the Humane Society. Besides, they don't belong to you. You can't do that!"

Sonia started to cry,

"I know you don't know your neighbor Margaret very well, but she's a psychologist. She might have an idea about what to do."

Margaret went straight to the intensive care unit. "I'd like to see my sister, Susan," she told the charge nurse.

"Of course! Right this way. You're her sister? No offense, but the two of you must be quite different in age."

"What do you mean?"

"Well, we have Susan's driver's license and it says she is 46, and, I'm sorry, you must be a bit older."

"Did you think I said sister? I said my sister's child. She's my niece. I don't hear very well."

The nurse looked her over skeptically. "Hmmm. Well, come this way. You might also want to know that some of her neighbors were here this morning inquiring after her."

"Thank you. I'll try to get over to Susan's house later and let them know how Susan is doing. How IS Susan doing?"

"I'll have the doctor stop by to speak with you."

Margaret was taken into the cubicle where Susan lay. She was attached to all kinds of tubes. Her eyes were closed. Her face was blotchy and bloated. She did not look well at all, but Margaret didn't know how she usually looked.

"Susan," Margaret said softly. There was no response. "Susan, it's me, Margaret." There was no response, likely because she was unconscious, but also because she didn't know who Margaret was. "Susan, you have to tell us what to do with your dogs!" Margaret whispered in Susan's ear. There was no response.

A doctor walked in. "Oh, we're so glad to have family here. We have very little information about Susan, and perhaps you can help give us some background."

The deer in the headlights.

"Oh! Of course. I'll help in any way I can, but we haven't been that close. I can call my sister if I can't answer your questions. I live in another state and just happened to be in town today."

After giving the physician quite a bit of undoubtedly false information, Margaret was able to learn that Susan had had a stroke, had nearly died, and had undergone emergency surgery. She was likely going to be hospitalized for quite some time. Margaret smiled weakly and stumbled out of the cubicle. She made it to her car and drove home, wondering if lying to a doctor was the same as lying to a police officer or a jury and whether or not she had jeopardized Susan's care in any way.

Over the next several days, a routine evolved for care of the dogs. All six dogs were taken to Susan's back yard during the day to eat the dog food and drink the water that Sonia provided for them, and to pee and poop to their heart's content. Mark had retrieved his lawnmower and nailed a board over the doggie door to keep the dogs outside. There was a round-up at suppertime when the dogs would be captured by dangling cookies at them, put in pet carriers and taken to the Bittlemeier garage. Sonia had Mark purchase one more pet carrier so that Lassie would no longer be a free agent. The dogs did not like this arrangement at all, and made a noticeable ruckus when the lights went out in the garage. Suspecting that Lassie was the leader of the bark chorus, Mark reluctantly brought her up to their bedroom in her pet carrier when they were ready to go to bed. But, Lassie was clearly used to sleeping with humans and pillows, and whined until they let her out. There was a measure of peace once they lifted her into bed with them. She showed an early preference for Sonia's feather pillow over Mark's foam rubber.

Mark enlisted Reuben's help, and they spent the weekend constructing a couple of large doghouses to put in Sonia's back yard so that the dogs could find shelter from the sun and weather. Dog food, leashes, a pet carrier, and doghouses. Ka-ching, ka-ching. Perhaps boarding them would be cheaper. He hoped they could learn to stay in Susan's back yard at night as well as during the day, but was satisfied to take it one step at a time.

Wendy and Margaret now joined Sonia in the mornings to get the dogs out of the garage and take them for a walk, two dogs each, before depositing them all in Susan's back yard. One morning, their parade passed Georgiana's house and she was out in front, standing behind a tree. She was wearing a full length flowing muumuu print dress, a cowboy hat and sunglasses. Her long white hair was braided and fell down her back. Wendy called out, "Good morning, Georgiana!" and continued walking. Sonia called out, "Good morning, Georgiana!" and continued walking. Margaret started to wave, squinted, hesitated for the slightest of moments, and then nodded and walked on by at the back of the pack without saying anything. She didn't know Georgiana, and she had two dogs on leashes pulling her forward.

Georgiana watched the three women and six dogs go by and raised her hand in greeting, but she too, said nothing.

This dream of Margaret's was about a live tiger, curled in the corner of the lobby at the mental health center. Someone informed her that it was there, and she had to go check for herself. Sure enough, it was there. She thought it might be wounded, but she didn't see anything obvious. As tigers go, this one was benign, sleepy even. She wondered if she should call the zoo to see if a tiger was missing. Then she remembered, this WAS the zoo. She couldn't find a phone number anyway. So, it was just her and the tiger and the person who told her it was there, someone who looked a lot like Tom Nickerson.

After the morning walk and the dogs were settled across the street, the three women would gather for coffee. What could they do with these dogs? How could they find out about Susan?

"Margaret, you have to go back and see how she's doing," pleaded Sonia.

"You've got to be kidding!" Margaret exclaimed.

"It's been almost a week. Surely she's awake by now! And, the staff will think you are not a good aunt if you don't visit more."

"I told them I lived out of state! I can't just stop by. It doesn't make sense."

"One last visit before going home," said Wendy. "Please. Sonia can't go on like this. Besides, maybe there will be entirely different staff on duty today.

Aunt Margaret knew her way now to the intensive care unit, and attempted to project a confidence that she did not feel as she approached the nursing station.

"Excuse me. I'd like to see my niece Susan one more time before I must leave town."

"Susan is no longer with us," said the nurse.

"What? She died?"

"No, no. I'm sorry. She's been moved to a private room on the cardiac floor. She's in room 314."

"Oh my goodness. So she's improving?"

"Why don't you visit with her care staff on the third floor?"

Margaret decided to just go to the third floor and enter Susan's room without asking anyone or lying to anyone about who she was. There didn't seem to be anyone in the immediate vicinity, and the door to Room 314 was ajar, so she slipped inside. Susan looked exactly the way she had looked a few days before in the intensive care unit, and her eyes were still closed.

"Susan," Margaret said softly. Susan did not move.

"Susan," Margaret repeated a bit more loudly.

Susan's eyes popped open.

"Susan, hello! Hello! How are you?"

"Who the hell are you?" Susan asked.

"I'm your neighbor, Margaret Sneed."

"I don't want to see anyone. Go away."

"It's about your dogs . . ."

Susan tried to sit up. "My dogs? What about my dogs? Where are they?"

"Your neighbor Sonia across the street has been taking care of them since you have been in the hospital. They aren't very friendly, except Lassie; she's getting easier to handle now."

"LASSIE? I don't have any dogs named Lassie!"

"Sonia didn't know their names, so they've all been given temporary names. You could help by giving me their names and making some suggestions for us about their care."

"How dare any of you touch my dogs!" Susan's face was turning bright red. Several of the machines attached to her began to whir and beep and flash lights. A nurse rushed in. She saw Margaret and told her she would have to leave. Margaret edged toward the door and was able to make her exit just as the doctor she had met previously entered the room. He turned to ask her a question but by then she was in the stairwell, lickety-split, headed for freedom.

"She's alive and she doesn't want us messing with her dogs."

"OK. Fine. Let's just put them back in her yard and take the plywood away from the doggie door. They can all go in the house and wait for her to come home."

"Yeah. Right. Like you'd do that."

"Seriously, she said not to mess with her dogs? What did she think had happened to them all this time?"

"I'm not sure she's been awake that long or knows how long she's been away from them."

"We could send her a note. And a bill. I've kept all our receipts."

"Sonia, Sonia, Sonia. This will all work out."

"Actually, if and when she does come home, I think I'll keep Lassie. She seems to like me, and maybe Susan wouldn't notice one missing."

"I'm pretty sure Susan can count to six."

Margaret, Sonia and Wendy were, once again, drinking coffee. They were seated on bar stools at the island dividing Sonia's kitchen from a more formal dining area. Lassie was curled up at Sonia's feet, but occasionally looked up at Sonia adoringly. Sonia was, after all, the heroine that had saved the day. The other five dogs were already across the street, running loose in Susan's back yard."

Margaret said, "Well, guess who called me this morning."

That got the others' attention. "Who?" they asked simultaneously.

"Susan! Susan called me."

"Susan? Well, then, we know she survived her Aunt Margaret's last visit! Was she nice, or is she still threatening us?'

"No, she seemed pretty rational. She asked who was taking care of the dogs and how they were doing. She did say, now that we were related (!), that she expected more assistance than she was getting."

"Ha! She didn't rat you out to the hospital staff?"

"Apparently not. I think she must realize what a bind she is in, being pretty helpless in regards to her dogs and her house and everything. Now that she has an 'aunt' in the area, she seems intent on making use of her. We had a fairly decent conversation until I told her we put the dogs in her back yard during the day. This really freaked her out, saying they needed careful supervision, that they should only go outside one at a time and not stay out more than a few minutes or they'd get too much sun or fleas or get dirty or be lonely. She warned us (you) to keep the 'girls' away from the 'boys' when they were in heat, as they were registered dogs and their reproduction was to be carefully planned and controlled in regards to who the daddy was for each mommy. She started getting worked up again, so I brought the conversation to a close, but not before leaving her your number, Sonia."

"Yikes! Thank you so much!"

"You're very welcome."

"No, seriously--do you think she'll call me? What can I say? That we're doing everything she told us not to do?"

"I think we're holding all the cards here. If she gets nasty, hang up."

"What if she insists on having us call them by their real names and feeding them a certain kind of food and grooming them and taking them to whatever dog shows she has lined up? What if she finds out the mommy and daddy doggies spend their entire days together, heat or no heat, doing whatever it is that doggies do?"

"Hey, you're the peacemaker here. You'll think of something. If you don't, just hang up. Anyway, you have caller ID, don't you?"

The doorbell rang. Wendy bounded down the stairs to see who was there. It was Margaret. She was standing in front of the door, holding onto a tree that was about her height, its roots tied in a burlap bag. It sported a few oddly shaped leaves. "I brought you this tree."

Wendy just stared at her.

"It's a ginkgo tree. You have sycamore trees and oak trees and maple trees and redbud trees. But you don't have a ginkgo tree. I thought you might like to have a ginkgo tree."

Wendy seemed perplexed by the offering and continued to stare at her.

"I was talking to Sonia yesterday," Margaret explained. "She was out in her yard with the dogs, and I asked her about her unusual tree. She told me that it was a ginkgo tree and that they had planted it in memory of their daughter Emmie. After I went home, I thought what a nice idea that was, and wondered if you might like to have a tree for Grace."

"Oh, my."

Margaret smiled and held the little tree out to her. Wendy smiled back. She reached out and grasped the small trunk, leaned forward and kissed one soft green leaf.

Wendy was gazing absentmindedly out the second floor window of her studio, when she was suddenly aware that it was time to pay attention to neon. In particular, she wanted to know how to make a ginkgo leaf out of neon, one that glowed yellow in the night. She was pretty sure Reuben wouldn't be crazy about the idea of affixing it to the front of the house, and wasn't even sure if it was legal, but her office space was her own, and she could put it in her window. "It's time," she thought.

Wendy found a place advertised on the internet that offered instruction in the neon process. Unfortunately, it was in London. She thought perhaps she could set this up in conjunction with one of Reuben's "State of the Map" conferences the next time it was held in London, but now that she had identified her next artistic adventure, she knew she wouldn't be able to wait. She was undaunted by the words of the London neon artist, Julia Bickerstaff, "Essentially, there are only three risks—cutting yourself, burning yourself and electrocuting yourself." Wendy couldn't wait!

There was a sign shop in town that had the word "neon" in its name, so that seemed like a good place to start. She was hoping that she could visit, watch a neon sign being made, get a list of the equipment she would need, buy it, and then make her neon leaf. Her contact with this agency resulted in the sad news that this business no longer produced neon signs. However, she was referred to an artist living within driving distance who might still be using neon in his business. She sent him an inquiry, but received no reply.

Maybe she would have to go back to school. She could go to an art school for a graduate degree. There, she could get good instruction in sculpture, with an emphasis on the art of neon. She was only in her early 50s. Was it too late? Wouldn't that take years? Would she even want or need a neon ginkgo leaf by then? Maybe, she could contact the local art center and see if anyone there had any ideas. Or, she could just look out the window a while longer.

"Why so glum, Wendy?" asked Reuben. They were eating frozen Girl Scout cookies in the stairwell.

"I want to know how to make neon, and I don't know how to start. The only viable contact I have lives in another town and isn't responding to me."

"Well, let's just go there and meet him," suggested Reuben. "If you show up at the business, you'd at least get to meet him and maybe something could come out of that."

And so, they did. They hopped in the car and headed south, looking for information and inspiration.

The business that was home to the alleged neon artist was in a non-descript building on the edge of a small town. The building was trying hard not to be noticed. There were no windows on the front. Two small words on the front door said, simply, "Sign Shop." Nothing about the place seemed to be interesting enough to solicit customers or clarify what the business was about except those two words. There was a car parked in front, but not much else going on anywhere in any direction.

"You would think a sign shop would have a real sign," said Wendy, somewhat apprehensively.

"You would think."

A middle-aged man was just coming out the door and turning to lock up the place when Wendy and Reuben pulled in alongside the one car in front of the building. He seemed surprised to see them, but his demeanor was open and friendly. Wendy got out of the car and introduced herself and Reuben. The man stepped forward and extended his hand. "Ben," he said. Wendy blurted out that she was interested in the neon process and wanted to see it being made and wondered if he still made neon and could she watch him sometime. He took note of her enthusiasm and smiled. He told her that yes, he still made neon signs, but no, she couldn't watch. He said he was a "one-man" operation, and that he needed quiet space in order to concentrate when he was working with glass and fire. He didn't like to be watched.

Wendy could understand this. She asked hopefully if, instead, she might come back sometime when he wasn't busy and just have him show her the equipment he used and walk her through the process. After she asked this, he paused for a moment, weighing that possibility, then smiled and said to them both, "Come on in." In that moment, he was transformed from a man unlocking a door into a neon artist, proud and passionate about his work. Wendy and Reuben went inside with him and entered a whole new world of light and color and history and artistry. Ben graciously allowed them to look around his office and his studio. The walls were hung with neon signs, and Wendy felt a rush of excitement as Ben turned the signs on, one by one. There was evidence everywhere of a lifetime of collecting and creating.

After they had soaked up the atmosphere, Ben showed them a sign on a work table that he had just started to make. They saw clear glass tubing that had been bent by fire and placed on a pattern, waiting for the next step. Ben then walked around showing them various pieces of equipment and describing the part each played. He showed them the Crossfire equipment he used for welding, and the ribbon fire he used to make circular bends. He showed them his manifold, vacuum pump and transformer. He explained that one needed to be both an artist and a scientist to create neon works. The art was in the designing of the patterns and the bending of the glass. The science was in making it glow.

Wendy was beginning to feel overwhelmed. "This isn't going to be as easy as I thought," she thought.

Ben continued to play his role as teacher. He told them that once the glass had been bent to match the pattern, electrodes would be put into each end. There was a hole in the electrode. A partial vacuum would be created and air would be sucked out of the tubing. Then, the electrodes would be attached to power and heated to 500°. This would purify the inside of the tube. Once there was a vacuum, the tube would be filled with argon or neon gas to the correct pressure. Argon gas would make a blue light, neon would make a red light. Ben said these were the only two colors of gas. To get other colors, one would start with tubes that had been pre-coated with florescent powder of different colors that would react with the gas.

Wendy's eyes glazed over.

About this time, she noticed his hands. "Ummm," she asked, "Have you ever been burned?"

He showed her the burn scars on his hands. "Sometimes," he said, "when you've been working on a piece in the fire for an hour and the choice is to stop heating it, knowing it will break, or keep going and get burned, you take the burn."

"Oh," she said.

Ben told Wendy that he had gone to "neon school" in Wisconsin over 30 years ago. He felt that after 5 years, he could make average neon signs, and after ten years, he thought he had become pretty good and knew what he was doing.

"Ten years?" Wendy could have fainted, right there in the glow of neon and argon.

Reuben had been following along with all of this, and could see that Wendy was backing away from the idea of becoming a neon artist. Still, he was curious, and asked Ben how his business was doing. Ben told them that he still had plenty of requests for neon signs, but that overall it was a dying art. He said it was getting more and more difficult to purchase supplies from fewer and fewer suppliers, and that he often had to order them in larger quantities than he needed in order to get them at all. Still, he said, he loved neon and would keep working with it as long as he could.

This spontaneous visit was helping Wendy realize that she would be an unlikely neon artist or neon scientist in her lifetime. Rather, she fell into the category of an unskilled but rabid neon art lover. She showed Ben her photograph of a ginkgo leaf and told him that was what she had wanted to make, a yellow ginkgo leaf, but was now doubting that she could ever be skilled enough to make it. She asked Ben if he would consider making it into neon for her. She thought the chances were that it might even look like a ginkgo leaf if Ben made it. He said he would think about it.

On the drive home, she was already shifting her thoughts to other possibilities for artistic expression.

Charity events bring interesting opportunities for givers to give money somewhat painlessly. When it's for a good cause, people often purchase items they don't really need, or participate in fundraising events that might not otherwise interest them. People might pay outrageous sums for decorated Christmas trees if the profits are going to help disabled children, attend festive Mardi Gras parties where donated masks of all kinds are put up for auction to benefit the local Art Center, or dress up and dance for dogs and cats. There are seasonal cookie sales by the Girl Scouts, popcorn sales by the Boy Scouts and mattress sales at the high school to raise money for the school band's trip to the Orange Bowl or to Tasmania. Whether for vanishing species, building homes for the homeless, or protecting the wilderness, there always seems to a grand idea for fundraising. If the pitch is right, the cause is plausible, the event catches the imagination or just sounds like fun, folks line up with their good intentions and their wallets.

Such was the case for "Cows on Parade," an imaginative fundraising phenomenon that had its origins in Zurich and quickly spread to cities all over the world. Life-sized cow shapes formed of fiberglass were transformed into works of art by local artists and placed in locations around a host city. Though bolted in place and certainly not mobile or in a row, these public art exhibits came to be called *parades*. The individual cows making up the cow parades were sponsored by local businesses and eventually auctioned off to raise money for local charities. "Cows on Parade" raised monies in Buenos Aires, London, and Tokyo, to name but a few.

Seattle took the "Cows on Parade" idea and changed it to "Pigs on Parade," bringing life to costumed pigs and raising over a million dollars for kids. In the college town of Lawrence, Kansas, the Jayhawk, the mythical mascot of the University of Kansas, was developed into its own parade. While any town could host a cow, only Lawrence could host a Jayhawk! Made of fiberglass like the cows, 30 of these giant birds were created, adopted by sponsors, turned over to artists, and adorned with all manner of fun names and fashionable attire, and then sold. "Jayhawks on Parade" raised $300,000 for local charities. Many of the birds still held their places years after the original events, providing whimsical backdrops for numerous amateur and professional photographs taken by university students and tourists, wedding parties and nostalgic alumni.

"Cows on Parade," "Pigs on Parade," and "Jayhawks on Parade" were outrageously fun events that were right up Wendy's alley. She first became aware of them when she and Reuben were in Chicago in 1999, just as their 300 cows were being put on parade. They saw "Muddy Holly and Peggy Sue" playing the piano and singing, two brown cows named "How" and "Now," and Odalisque, a red cow with its feet (and udder) pointed to the sky, posed on a corner near a bus stop and subtitled "Reclining Nude." Wendy was so enamored by the largeness of the idea, the wonderful inventiveness of it all, that she talked her mother into making visits to these parades with her whenever one was being held in an interesting location. The parades provided a way for the two of them to spend enjoyable time together, courtesy of her mother's pocketbook. They had racked up an impressive collection of cow parades, including New York City, Kansas City, Boston, Austin and Detroit. They had also visited some of the spin-off parades and had gone to Seattle for the pigs, Tulsa for penguins and

Lawrence for the Jayhawks. They hadn't yet had a chance to visit an international parade, but Wendy thought she would go in a heartbeat if she could have Reuben as her companion instead of her mother, due to his knowledge of maps and the romance inherent in foreign travel. For the time being, the domestic adventures with her mother gave Wendy plenty to think about. As a new parade location loomed on the horizon, she and her mother would plot out an excursion as a several-day mini-vacation. They would make sure to find and admire the entire collection of sculptures, and supplement the parades with visits to art museums and good restaurants. Wendy photographed each cow, each pig, each penguin and each Jayhawk, storing her photographs of these works of art in albums and cataloging them in her mind for future use.

The idea of creating a parade of sculptures of some type had stayed with Wendy for years. She didn't know how to make them. She didn't know how to fund them. She didn't know how to decorate them, who would buy them, or why. But, in the back of her mind, there was a parade. The subject would be worked out at a later date. The details would be determined at a later date. Everything was stored away, waiting.

And then, Susan's dogs came into her life.

A parade of dachshunds?

Why not?

In her imagination, Wendy could see some of them already. As the main attraction, as the star of the exhibit, there would be a long, low, brown dachshund with a great golden mane: Lassie. The idea of a Lassie dachshund always gave her a chuckle. She wondered if dachshunds and collies had ever interbred. Probably not. But, art is art, and anything the mind could create was fair game. In Wendy's "Parade of Dachshunds," there could be a short, green, ferocious-looking "Pup the Magic Dragon," a "Hot Dach" in a bun, a "doG" in a long white robe, maybe with a halo or brandishing lightning bolts. What clothing store wouldn't want a stylish "Putting on the Dog" out front, wearing a red satin gown and lots of diamond jewelry, or wearing a tuxedo and a top hat? There would definitely be an Itsy Bitsy Teeny Wienie in a yellow polka dot bikini. Darn! She wished she could draw better. She wished she knew more about various sculpting techniques. She wished she could create a display that would make other people laugh. How could she make this happen?

While Wendy's town had hosted a parade, it had happened a long time ago. Maybe her very own town was ready for a new parade. Maybe they were just waiting for her and her ideas. Maybe the time was right for "Dachshunds on Parade!"

Wendy had read that the town's original parade had been sponsored by the city's Convention and Visitor's Bureau, local businesses and the university. She was too intimidated to contact someone at the university, but thought someone at the Convention and Visitor's Bureau might be willing to talk with her. She decided to stop by their office and see if anyone who worked there had been part of the original parade. Their office was housed in a little attachment to the town's Carnegie Library. Someone with a sense of architectural design had actually managed to make this new addition to an old building look like it belonged there. Wendy scoped it out, took a deep breath, and went inside.

"Hello. I'm trying to find someone who worked on the charity parade, "she told the friendly receptionist. "Are any of those folks still around?"

A staff member at another desk heard her question, got up and came over to Wendy.

"I was there," she said. "What do you need to know?"

"I was thinking about the idea of another parade, and needed some details about the one you already had."

"Well, I was just getting ready to go for a coffee. Would you like to join me? We could talk then."

They crossed over to a little coffee shop, each got a cup, and found a quiet booth at the back.

"Now, how can I help you?" asked Wendy's coffee companion.

"I was thinking about setting up a Parade of Dachshunds. Don't you think that would be fun? You had fun with your parade, didn't you?"

"Yes, it was fun," her coffee companion said in answer to Wendy's first question. "It was fun for me personally, fun for all of us who participated in putting it together, and fun for the many citizens and visitors who came to see it. Is that what you would be going for? Fun?"

"Well, yes, sort of," admitted Wendy. "I thought I'd like to use art to make people laugh."

"Hmmm. That seems like a lot of work for a laugh. For me, it was fun, but it was also like having a second full-time job for seven or eight months."

"What kind of work are you talking about? I'm not afraid of work."

"I'm sure you would work very hard, and you would need to, in order to pull it off. The first hurdle would be in convincing the city that another parade would be a good idea. Then, you'd need to identify sponsors and artists. Someone would need to design a three dimensional model of a dachshund that would be used in making the fiberglass molds. You'd need to figure out transportation for them. You'd need to know how much they would weigh and what kind of base they'd need to be bolted to—you know, heavy enough to keep from being stolen, and a sturdy weight that could withstand wind without snapping the form from its base. You'd need cement. Lots of cement."

"Cement."

"Yes. We got all of our cement donated."

"Donated cement."

"Who else is on your committee, by the way?"

"Committee?"

"Yes, do you have a committee? You know, contacts in the community who can help with all aspects of the parade."

"I don't have a committee."

"Have you talked with anyone else about this? I mean, how do you know your community would even be amenable to having big dachshunds everywhere? Are there little dachshunds everywhere? I mean, is this area some kind of a mecca for dachshunds? I suppose the idea could catch on if the city was going to host a national dachshund convention, or something like that."

"We have six dachshunds on our block."

Wendy's coffee companion smiled. "That's a good beginning."

"I just thought people would think it was fun and would want to see the parade."

"People probably would think it was fun, but a lot would have to happen first, and there's no way one person could do something like this alone. You would need to collaborate. You would need all kinds of expertise, and different personality types who could look at things from different points of view and help problem-solve. And what about the money? You'd have to have such a good idea that people would be willing to give money to make it happen."

"I have money. Well, I don't have money, but I have access to money."

"I don't mean to sound discouraging, but I think money or no money, you would need people. And, you'd need a purpose. The parades that have been put on everywhere have had the support of their communities because they increase tourism and have a positive economic impact. People come to see the exhibit because the pieces are beautiful works of art, created usually by a wide variety of talented and clever artists. And, when people come, the money follows. There is also the noble purpose of using them to raise money for charities. Would your Parade of Dachshunds have any kind of noble purpose? You'd need to research all of this before you got too far along."

"I think making people laugh is noble."

"I do agree with that. But to put on a city-wide event, you would still need to pair that hoped-for laugh with an economic benefit to the city or to some segment of the city's population, and you would need influential contacts in the form of people."

"Well, Christo, that artist who put orange gates all over Central Park in New York City, was just making art for art's sake. It didn't raise money for any noble purpose. It probably did boost tourism for New York City, but I think its main purpose was to take people's breath away. It was just beautiful. And he could do it because he was rich and he was persistent. He had big dreams, and realizing his dreams made him happy!"

"And," her companion said, "It worked because he was Christo." She didn't know what else to say. She didn't want to convey her honest assessment that Wendy's idea was doomed, but she believed it was.

"Wendy," she said as she stood and gathered her things, "Good luck!"

Wendy left the coffee shop and headed home. Once again she was startled by the huge chasm that always seemed to form between having a grand idea and the execution of it. She thought her coffee companion was right. She needed people to help her for something big like a city-wide art exhibit. As she drove, somewhat absentmindedly, pausing at yellow lights, stopping at red lights, going on green lights, she wondered if she would pursue her parade idea. That got her to thinking about the word *parade*. Cow parade. Pig parade. Were these really parades? No. They weren't. That was a stupid name. If anything, these exhibits were "Parades of People." There were stationary works of art scattered around a city. They had a central theme that bound them together, but they didn't move. These forms themselves were not the parade. The actual parade was of the people who moved around to look at them. The forms had the theme, the people had the parade.

"How was your coffee and conversation about a Parade of Dachshunds, Wendy," asked Reuben when he got home that evening.

"Oh, Reuben. The conversation was pretty discouraging."

"Tell me about it."

"I think I'm going to have to stick with real live dachshunds for now. I don't know enough people and I don't have enough of an artistic reputation to even begin to think about such a project. The conversation did get me to thinking about parades, though. You know, anything could be considered a parade if you looked at it as a collection with a central theme that *people* paraded around to see. I mean, realtors are always showcasing a parade of homes. That's just not accurate. The homes don't move, they are identified as homes for sale, and the people who are interested in homes, parade through them and either buy them or they don't. If you think about it, anything that involved moving people could be considered a parade. Maybe people would parade through *our* neighborhood. You could make a map, Reuben! And people could walk along our sidewalks and admire us! Each of us is unique. The houses we live in, the clothes we wear, the things that interest us. We could attract a parade of people."

After this long response to Reuben's question, and as he puzzled over her logic, she started to cry. "Anyway," she said. "I've decided to give up art. I'm going to be a writer.

Sonia was in the basement, looking for her old Singer sewing machine. She practically tripped over some cords hanging out of a box of computer parts that had been deposited at the bottom of the stairs. Good grief! Why was that there? She looked around. Egads. How had they acquired so much junk? She and Mark were going to have to take a serious look at the accumulation of boxes of letters and old teaching materials and broken furniture and partially used cans of paint and framed posters and wrapping paper and tools and vacuum cleaner parts and old bedding that cluttered nearly every square inch of their basement. After the serious looking, some serious time would need to be invested in clearing out years of solving space problems upstairs by carting whatever it was to this graveyard downstairs. She found the sewing machine. Yuck. It was covered with a greasy dust. She wondered how long it had been since she used it, and thought it had probably been some Halloween costume for one of the kids. So, a long time ago. She wasn't even sure it worked any more, but she lugged it upstairs and put it on the dining room table. "Well," she thought. "This could be the start of something big."

"Reuben, why do you think Jesus was God's only begotten son? I mean, he is God, right? Couldn't he beget as many sons as he wanted? Or, how about begetting a daughter? It would only be fair!"

Wendy and Reuben were sitting in their stairwell, having one of their talks.

"Well, that's an interesting question. Maybe he felt he got it right the first time. Maybe he thought he had made his point, and one was enough. Your parents thought one was enough. You, did, too."

"Yeah. Still . . ."

They sat quietly for a while, Wendy sitting on the top step, Reuben slouched halfway down.

"Reuben, are you disappointed in me?"

"What do you mean?"

"I thought maybe you thought you were marrying someone who would be a real artist, maybe even famous, and I'm not, and I just wondered if you were disappointed."

"The short answer is, no, I never had expectations that you would be a famous artist, but if you had been, I'd have been happy for you. And, who knows what is ahead? Let me ask you this, are you disappointed that I'm an ordinary map-maker?"

"I've never thought about that. The difference is that you can see I'm not a successful artist. How would I know if you messed up some longitude or latitude or put some town in the wrong country?"

He laughed.

"Wendy, you aren't an ordinary person. I love it that you express yourself in so many ways. I love being constantly surprised by your interests."

"That's a nice thing to say. You know, Reuben, you should really be the one living on the second floor."

"What?"

"You are much nicer, and much closer to heaven than I am. If it turns out that you are right and there is an afterlife, will you put in a good word for me?"

"I'm sure I wouldn't have any clout, but I do know it wouldn't be heaven without you."

"See what I mean? You're just nice! Are you sure you want to go to this place you believe is there? What do you imagine it will be like? I mean, everyone just sitting around in awe? Like being in a spell of some sort? I just don't get how that would work. I mean, would Grace be there? What about Grace's father? What about his wife and his other children? It seems like it would just be constantly awkward."

"I don't think personal relationships are what it is all about. Rather it would be like a state of happiness for everyone."

"How would that be better than being able to touch someone right here, right now, or being able to hear them laugh, or tasting chocolate or seeing the full moon come up over the horizon or seeing the color magenta or standing in the dark and hearing the sound of ice melting off the roof?"

"Oh, Wendy. I suppose heaven could be all of those things at the same time, and more."

"I don't think I want to eat chocolate while ice is melting on my head."

"Well, no . . ."

Georgiana was outside. It was a cool fall day. She sat on her porch step and watched the clouds arrange themselves in new ways. "Could rain," she thought.

"Tom?"

Georgiana was startled out of her reverie. Margaret was down on the sidewalk looking up at her.

"Tom Nickerson?"

Georgiana froze.

"Tom, you may not remember me, but I was a psychologist. Many years ago you came to see me. I believe you had suffered a loss. I always wondered how you were doing. In fact, I had a dream about you just recently."

"Is that a fact."

"You know, I've lived in this neighborhood going on twenty years, and I never knew you were my neighbor."

"I saw you once or twice up the street."

"Yeah. I live just up the way. I'm retired now. I thought I'd plant some trees in my front yard to remind me about my boys. I never see them anymore."

"Is that a fact."

"That is a fact. A sad but true fact. The last time I saw you, your wife had just died, and I always felt bad that you didn't come back to talk more about that."

"That was a long time ago."

"Yes, it was. I'm thinking it was twenty or so years ago. What was your wife's name?"

After a long pause, he said, "Georgiana. Her name was Georgiana."

"That's a beautiful name. I was talking to Wendy across the street and she asked me if I knew you. Then I had that dream. Then I remembered you."

"Hmmm."

"I got some ginkgo trees from Mark, down at the nursery. They're small ones. I bought four. One for each of my boys, one for Wendy, and this one for you, for your wife, if you'd like to have it."

"A ginkgo tree."

"Yes, kind of a remembrance tree."

"Is that what Wendy just planted?"

"Yes."

"Why'd she plant one?"

"For a child she lost, a long time ago."

"So we'd have a whole grove up and down the street."

"Yes. We'd have these pretty little trees standing in for those we've lost who aren't here anymore. We'd also have color and shade and something in common."

"Hmmm . . ."

Sonia sat at her sewing machine. After finally finding it in their junked-up basement, she had taken it upstairs, set it up on the dining room table and plugged it in. She had thought she wanted to make a vest with pockets for weighted beanbags, as an experiment in managing her weight. She had shopped for a pattern for vests, but couldn't find one with the necessary number of pockets (10), so she would have to improvise adding pockets all over. She wasn't a wearer of vests, and, when it came right down to it, she couldn't imagine wearing one around the house, let alone out in public, so she didn't buy a vest pattern. A jacket seemed like a better alternative. She did wear jackets and thought with a jacket, there would be more room for pockets, and she would be more likely to wear it. So, she had shopped for, found and purchased a pattern for a jacket. The pattern allowed for two pockets, so she would have to figure out how to add eight more.

Sonia had gotten far enough along in her plan to locate and set up her sewing machine and to purchase a pattern for a jacket. Going forward with the project was the problem. It was summer, and realistically she didn't think she'd wear a jacket in the summer. She was wearing t-shirts. The thought of wearing a t-shirt with ten pockets, hopefully stuffed with beanbags was nothing short of ridiculous. She had the jacket pattern. Maybe she'd just practice making a jacket and worry about where the weights would go after it was made. She could decide then if she'd really wear it.

Sonia had found and ordered some adorable material for a jacket. It was covered in dachshunds. In fact, it was so cute, she thought she'd probably want to wear such a jacket in public, and not have the strange bulges from weighted beanbags here and there making her look even bulgier herself than she was. The material was on its way. She sat at her sewing machine, took the jacket pattern out of its envelope and sighed. She didn't like it any more. All in all, her weight loss project seemed too complex to initiate. Maybe she could use the material she had ordered to make shopping bags. She could make one for Wendy and Margaret, and perhaps even Susan. She would need a pattern.

One day Reuben pulled up in the driveway and saw an extension ladder propped up against the house. Wendy was sitting two stories up, on the roof.

"What in God's name are you doing up there?" he shouted.

"I'm taking down this goddamned weather vane!" she shouted back.

"Wendy! Come down! You're going to fall!"

"I'll come down when I figure out how to take this weather vane off."

"Why are you doing that?"

"I've never liked it."

"I thought you thought it was funny."

"I did think it was funny when we first moved here, and all the houses got one as they were finished. But now I resent the fact that the arrow is supposed to be directed at someone's idea of where heaven is."

"Wendy, it's in the covenant in our homeowners' contract that each house will have a weather vane. You can't take it down."

"Reuben, we've lived here over 20 years. There are no Covenant Police."

"Wendy, it's just a weather vane. Besides, everyone thinks heaven is 'up there'."

Reuben regretted having said this, as soon as it was out of his mouth. Wendy never went for "everyone" and didn't include herself in that total.

"Well, I think heaven is right down here, and I don't want a weather vane telling me what I believe."

"Don't you think you could try to stop reading something into that hopeless piece of metal?"

"Reuben. I'm taking it down. You don't have to watch."

He went inside, but not before noticing that Sonia was standing in her driveway watching this exchange. In fact, it seemed to be a good show for several neighbors up and down the street. Later that week, he noticed that many other weather vanes had disappeared from rooftops on their block.

Margaret left the little ginkgo tree on the sidewalk after speaking with Tom, and walked back up the hill to her house. Tom had been jolted by her visit. He hadn't heard his name spoken out loud in twenty years. In his profound grief, he had transformed himself so completely into Georgiana that even he had forgotten life as Tom. So many years had gone by, so many years of trying to give life back to his wife by giving up his own.

Tom didn't know what to do with the tree. It was blocking the sidewalk for anyone out and about. He already had a lot of trees. He didn't need any more shade, and he certainly didn't need more places for squirrels to gather and complicate his counting routines. On the other hand, he didn't have a ginkgo tree and he didn't have a remembrance tree. A remembrance tree. Now, what was it he supposed to remember? No, who was it he supposed to remember? He continued to sit for a while on his front steps, staring at the tree and trying to find some order to his thoughts.

Already, the day was falling into evening. The light was changing. Slowly, he became aware that something was happening inside him, too, breaking loose. The horses on the hill were gathering in his memory, gathering and coming his way. There was a fence. He remembered the fence. He remembered reaching out. Maybe there was an answer in the air, just beyond his fingertips. As if in a trance, he stood and walked into the house, leaving the tree where it was. He went into the bathroom and looked at himself in the mirror for a long time.

"Tom," he said.

He took some scissors from the drawer and started cutting off swatches of his long white hair. When most of it was clipped short, he found a razor and shaved his head completely. Then, startled by his appearance, he started to cry. He remembered her and he missed her and he cried.

Tom and Georgiana had been married in a little chapel in the Ozarks. Her father and two sisters came, and both of Tom's parents were there. Tom's lab colleague who had provided the double date that led to their brief courtship, served as Tom's best man. Both of Georgiana's sisters stood up for her. Georgiana walked down the aisle on her father's arm, wearing a simple white gown and veil. The sight of her nearly took Tom's breath away. The small wedding party gathered afterward for dinner at a local restaurant, where the employees gathered around them and sang Happy Birthday to them, even though it wasn't anyone's birthday. Georgiana got a free dessert. It came with eight spoons.

Tom thought back to their first apartment. They had set up housekeeping on the second floor of a brick apartment building not far from Tom's lab. Georgiana was just twenty years old, and had not lived away from home before. She was ecstatic to have her own space and her own husband. Tom remembered her excitement over the towels and dishes and throw pillows and posters she acquired. Who got happy about towels? This was a whole new world to him. He was happy because she was happy.

Georgiana always jumped up and hugged him when he came in. She wasn't a great cook, but made them lots of macaroni and cheese and tuna salad. She especially liked sliced bananas with mandarin oranges, so they had that often.

Tom encouraged Georgiana to enroll in the local community college and she did. He would come home from work and see her sitting at their small kitchen table with class papers spread all about. Sometimes they did her homework together. They made it through English 101, Biology, American History and all the others. Tom hadn't remembered those classes being fun when he took them himself, but they seemed fun when she took them. Some days, he was able to walk her to class. He always carried her books. Other times, he would sit on a wall outside and wait for one of her classes to end. She would light up when she saw him there. Georgiana got her associate's degree and took a job as a school secretary at an elementary school not far from where they lived. They talked about starting a family and joked that their children would be giants and probably end up as basketball players since the two of them were so tall and thin.

He remembered those special early years of their life together. Contentment had set in, and the years went by. Somewhere in that stretch of years, their parents died, and Georgiana's two sisters did, as well. Was it cancer? He couldn't remember. Ten years of marriage came and went, and then twenty. They decided to buy a real house and talked with a builder who was just starting a development he was calling Heavenly Heights. They signed a contract and got a loan. They got to choose from among several house styles, floor plans, paint colors, tile. Georgiana had always wanted a garden. She was looking forward to planting bushes and flowers and getting new towels. Their house was to be the first on the block to be built. But, what happened? Suddenly she was sick. And almost as suddenly, she died. Bam!

Where did their life go? Where did it go? They were busy having a good life, and then, they weren't. Tom got lost. He got so lost. His work friends reached out to him for a time, but he quit his job and they drifted away. Georgiana's friends were devastated. They called, took him cakes and casseroles, but they gradually faded away, too, and he was alone.

Tom wallowed around in these old memories, but after a while, he felt much better. He went to the basement and rummaged around until he found an old pair of his jeans, a t-shirt and a ball cap. He dressed and went directly to the garage for a shovel. It took him a long time to dig a hole because it was dark and the ground was dry and hard. He kept at it. He wasn't thinking about chiggers. He hooked up the hose and filled the hole with water. While the water settled in the hole he had dug, he looked up at his neighbors' houses. Lights were on in most of them, and he imagined the inhabitants were sitting around tables eating their supper or watching the news together or reading. His gaze landed on the little ginkgo tree, sitting in its burlap bag on the sidewalk, waiting for him to claim it. And so, he did. He picked it up tenderly and carried it to the hole he had made and placed it inside. He sat on the ground and filled dirt in around the roots a handful at a time, patting it, patting it, patting it until it was firmly planted. He watered it one more time, put the hose and shovel away, sat on his porch and looked at this little tree, this special gift from a neighbor. The ginkgo leaves rustled slightly in the breeze and caught a bit of light from a rising moon.

"Georgiana," he said.

Sonia was sitting on her porch. Lassie was on a leash exploring some very interesting dirt under the bushes. The sun was up, but it was still quite early, and the neighborhood was quiet and peaceful. Before long, she would be getting all the dogs ready to go across the street for the day. While she was slowly formulating this plan in her head, the front door across the street opened and one of its occupants burst out of the door and bounded down his front steps. He had on running shorts and a t-shirt, as well as a determined look on his face. As he headed down his driveway toward the street, Sonia raised her hand in a greeting and called out, "Good morning!" He waved back, started to run, then circled around and trotted up her driveway.

"Hi. Is that your dog?"

"No. I'm taking care of it for a while for our neighbor, Susan."

"We had noticed a lot of dog activity in the neighborhood."

"Yeah. There are six of them! Their owner had a stroke. She's in the hospital. Do you know her? Susan?"

"Not at all. I didn't even know she wasn't at home. So, you're keeping her dogs for her?"

"She didn't ask us to. I just happened to take them and now I just happen to have them here. My husband thinks it's crazy for us to have these six dogs, and I have to admit, it's a lot of work. The best part of it is that I really like this one," she said, gesturing to Lassie, "and I'm getting more exercise than I have in years."

"I had a dachshund when I was growing up."

"Really? They're such funny looking things. What was your dog's name?"

"Sparky. He was a great dog."

"Do you have any pets now?"

"No. We're not home during the day, so it wouldn't seem fair."

"Well, for now anyway, we put all six dogs in Susan's back yard during the day. It's like a big doggie park for them. I couldn't imagine having them all in the house all day."

"When will Susan be home?"

"It's hard to say. I don't think she's in very good health. We need to decide what to do long term."

"You're a good neighbor."

"A crazy one! I've seen you and your housemate running a lot. How far do you run every day, anyway?"

"We run 4-6 miles a day. A bit more when we're training for a marathon."

"Wow. I probably walk 4-6 miles in a month. I do envy your passion and your commitment. I need to do something or I'll end up like Susan."

"You wouldn't have to run. Walking is good. Just add a little more each day and pretty soon, you'd be hooked. You should come to the walk/run that our running club is sponsoring next weekend to raise money for cystic fibrosis. You could start with a short walk that way and help for a good cause. Maybe you'd like it enough to keep it up."

"I'll think about it, if you'll think about taking one of these dogs."

He laughed. "Well, I must admit, seeing the dog is what made me stop for a minute. I could talk to Mike about it. We both do like dogs. My name is Stan, by the way."

"I'm Sonia."

"Have a good day, Sonia!" Stan smiled and ran backwards down the driveway, turned with a wave, and was off down the street. Sonia's chat with him perked her up quite a bit, and having a good day now seemed like a real possibility.

Margaret invited Bruce to go to the local theater production of *Jesus Christ Superstar* to celebrate her 70th birthday. They hadn't had a real date for many, many years, but he accepted and they went. As she watched it, she remembered some of the songs from having seen the production once in the past, and they were sung very well. However, she had forgotten how grim the production was. The dancers flitting through from time to time in their brightly colored outfits provided some oddly juxtaposed respite from the ancient story unfolding so sadly behind them. Other than that, she was waiting for the cast to drop their costumes in the finale, as they had in the production she had seen before. They didn't. They all wore white choir robes as they sang the last song.

"Well, I guess they didn't have enough nerve to appear nude in this production," she said to Bruce as they joined the exodus.

"Nude?"

"Yes! The last time I saw this, the cast all dropped their costumes at the end."

"Margaret. You are thinking of *Hair*, not *Jesus Christ Superstar!*" said Bruce, laughing.

"What? Oh my goodness, you're right! I wouldn't have come if I'd remembered that."

They walked together to Bruce's car and climbed into the front seat.

"Bruce," Margaret said, hesitantly. "It is funny that I got *Hair* and *Jesus Christ Superstar* mixed up. But, it also reminds me that I've been worried about my memory.

Sometimes I think I remember things accurately from a long time ago, but sometimes I can't remember something at all and feel confused. Do you think I'm losing it?"

"I think turning 70 tends to make one worry about every lapse in memory and judgment. I don't see you every day, but when I have seen you, I don't think I've noticed anything out of the ordinary. You do know that I'm Brad Pitt, right?"

She punched him on the arm and they started home.

Susan Cochran was born in 1970 in Detroit to wealthy parents who made their fortune in the automobile industry. She attended private schools her entire life. It is said that she was valedictorian of her high school class, thanks to grades that were already good, but may have been enhanced due to large donations made to the school by her parents. Susan was stand-offish in school and was not well-liked by her classmates or by faculty. She was fairly adept at insulting others' intelligence, appearance, genes, etc., and seemed to like life best when withdrawn into her own thoughts. Her only attachments as she grew up were to piano and to the family pets.

The Cochrans had purchased the largest Steinway grand piano available, primarily for show in their quite large and quite grand home, even though there were no known musicians in either family tree. Susan plunked on it as a toddler, and found herself drawn more and more to it as she got older. It seemed that she had somehow been born with musical ability. Her parents did take notice of this and acquired the best piano teachers for her as her proficiency increased. In fact, they were glad to turn Susan's time over to him for intensive instruction and practice, as they didn't really know how to relate to her or spend time with her. The bond that usually developed between parents and their children had not occurred in this case. Susan's parents had no interest in her, and even less interest in classical music. They rarely, if ever, attended one of her lessons or recitals. Susan didn't seem to notice. She could get lost in music while other children her age were out climbing trees, roller-skating or having pajama parties.

Susan had a brother, Philip, some five years younger who seemed to have preferred status within the family. He was a friendly kid who liked sports and was easier to relate to than she was. He was involved in soccer, played hockey, loved to water ski and could always be found hanging out with other kids who had time on their hands and money to spend.

Susan's parents were smokers and drinkers and partiers, leaving their progeny at home with the housekeeper, cook or piano teacher (in Susan's case), or with coaches at the Sport's Club (in Philip's case), while they engaged in social activities and even while they took lengthy cruises or trips abroad. During their absences, the two siblings spent quite a bit of time devising ways to make life more difficult for each other. Sheet music, hockey sticks and homework disappeared. Bugs and spiders were dropped inside shirts. Messages of importance were not passed along. Yelling, screaming and occasional physical altercations filled the empty spaces. If it hadn't been for the house staff intervening, neither child would have survived into adulthood.

Susan was in college and her brother still at home when they received word that their parents were listed as missing while on a Mediterranean cruise. These siblings would have found it difficult to say it mattered much to them, as they had never felt they mattered much to their parents. Unfortunately, their "missing" status meant years of legal uncertainty for Susan and Philip. When there was no sign of them after seven years, they were declared legally dead. Susan always believed that they just didn't want to come home and had figured out a way to live well somewhere else.

Susan was just twenty-five years old when she and her brother inherited the family home and their parents' fortune. Susan found out later that her brother had inherited not only half the estate, but was also the sole beneficiary on quite a hefty life insurance plan. She was wealthy, but he was really, really wealthy. If she hadn't disliked him before, she certainly did then. After the house was sold and the proceeds divided, she never spoke to him again. She had finished a degree in Art History while the estate was in limbo, and worked for a while in a museum office. She had her own cubicle. After the estate was settled, she quit her job. This was the only job she ever had. Her departure surprised some of her officemates, as they hadn't even known she worked there.

Susan bought a house of her own in Heavenly Heights. She could have afforded a much more expensive house in a much more expensive neighborhood, but preferred keeping a low profile. Instead, she spent her money on art work, good music, books, a grand piano and expensive show dogs. She bought a red Mercedes convertible that she kept in her garage and hadn't driven it since she brought it home. She had a van that she did drive, as she could transport all of her dogs in it at the same time. The interest from her diversified portfolio allowed her to do whatever she wanted to do, but she never wanted to do much, so her value increased substantially as time went on. Her best friend was her broker. He called her on a regular basis regarding various investments. To him, she was the goose that had laid the golden egg.

Susan's stroke had occurred in late spring, and by mid-summer, she was still not home. Though Margaret had given Sonia's phone number to Susan after her one visit to her at the hospital, Susan had never called Sonia and no one had been back to visit her. Her status was a mystery.

The neighbors were becoming increasingly worried about having an apparently abandoned house on the block. There was no activity at the house at all. It was dark at night, and seemed even darker somehow during the day. The only activity there was when the dogs were in the back yard. The dandelions had proliferated in the warmer weather and the crabgrass had taken hold. What grass that grew was long and in need of mowing. Windy days had scattered sticks and a few limbs about. Some of Georgiana's square chigger catchers still stuck to the west side of the house.

At some point, Susan's mailbox had become so stuffed that nothing else could fit inside. Sonia could see this every time she retrieved her own mail, but didn't know whether it was up to the neighbors to inform the post office of Susan's situation, or whether mail could or should be forwarded to a hospital. While she wondered about the propriety of doing this, she took it upon herself to begin collecting Susan's mail every few days in a cardboard box. She knew she would have to let Susan know she was doing this, or, God forbid, take it to her. Sonia didn't know how Susan's bills were getting paid and didn't want to know.

Mark began mowing Susan's yard. He liked a neat yard, and he didn't like seeing one falling into disrepair, especially one across the street where he could see it all the time. One evening, he went over and picked up sticks and litter. While he was there, he decided to mow it, just once. He thought the grass could use a hit or two of fertilizer. And water. It needed water. And, so, he was hooked. Susan's yard became a rehabilitation project for him. He took hoses and sprinklers over. His mowing, fertilizing and watering over the weeks made a big difference in the yard's appearance. When he thought about it, he couldn't remember how Susan's yard work had ever been done in the past. She must have had some kind of lawn service, because he sure had never seen her do any outside work herself. It had never been an especially attractive yard, but at least the basics had always been taken care of by somebody. Mark brought home a few pots of red geraniums from the nursery and put them up by the door. He got a ladder and took down the sticky chigger traps. He straightened up the junk in the back yard and could be seen, from time to time, throwing balls to the dogs to catch.

"This place could use some paint," he thought.

When six weeks' worth of mail filled the cardboard box that Sonia kept it in, she knew she would have to take it to Susan. Everyone was wondering in some vague way, how Susan was doing—not because they knew her and cared about her—but because they wanted things to be back to normal. Normal was a house with Susan in it, and not interacting, rather than not in it and not interacting. Her absence had generated more attention to her than her presence had. And now, it seemed, quite a few neighbors had become involved in her life because of her absence, caring for her dogs, mowing her yard, and speculating about her future.

Sonia, Wendy and Margaret decided they would go to the hospital as a united front to find out how Susan was doing and when she would be home. If Susan wouldn't speak to them, they would just have to demand some sort of information from a social worker or somebody in the know. How could someone with no connections just go on and on without somebody somewhere reaching out to solve the multiple problems that arose during long hospitalizations?

"We don't have a patient here by that name," said the hospital volunteer at the reception desk.

"Where is she?" asked Margaret.

"We don't have patient information here. You could try speaking with someone in admissions, but you might get more information if you spoke to the head nurse on her floor."

"And where would we find such a person," asked Margaret.

"What floor was she on the last time you saw her?"

"She was on the 3rd floor."

"Just take the elevator up to the third floor and ask someone at the nurses' station if you can talk to the head nurse."

They took the elevator to the third floor, went to the nurse's station and asked to speak to the head nurse.

She turned out to be the exact same person who had ushered "Aunt" Margaret to Susan's bedside in the intensive care unit. Darn! What was she doing up there?

Margaret pushed Sonia forward and tried to be invisible.

"We're here to ask about Susan Cochran," said Sonia.

"Susan Cochran is no longer our patient," the nurse informed them. She looked over this trio of visitors and spotted Margaret. "Oh, you are her aunt, if I remember correctly."

"Uh, yes."

"Well, then, Susan has been moved to a rehabilitation center. You are the only relative who visited or called in the time she was here, so you should know she suffered another stroke and is now having difficulty walking and talking. I'm sure it would do her good if you would try to visit her more frequently."

"Oh, dear. Where has she been taken now?"

The nurse gave her a card with the address and phone number of the local rehabilitation center, smiled curtly and walked away.

"So. What do you think? Shall we go check things out there?" Margaret asked the other two.

"What have we got to lose?"

The rehabilitation center was a rambling series of light brick buildings in a campus-type setting. They saw one building with a sign saying "Office," so parked the car and went inside. They inquired about Susan and were directed to one of the living units.

Susan was sitting in a wheelchair, looking out a window. The three neighbors approached her, Wendy carrying the box of mail.

"Susan, hello, how are you doing?" asked Margaret.

Susan turned her head slightly to look at them but showed no sign of recognition.

"Look, Susan, I've brought you your mail," said Sonia, holding out the box.

Susan made no move to take it from her, nor did she seem to be curious about what all was there, or why this stranger was bringing it to her.

"Susan, the nurse at the hospital told us you had had another stroke. We're very sorry to hear that," said Margaret. "The neighbors all told us to tell you they hope you are doing better and will be home soon."

Susan cocked her head and looked at them.

"We're taking care of your dogs and your yard. We hope that's OK," said Wendy.

"Mark put some red geraniums up by your front door. They look really nice," said Sonia.

Susan didn't say anything.

A staff person approached them. "I see you are here to visit Susan. That's so good! Isn't it, Susan?" he said, turning to look at Susan, who didn't answer. "Are you relatives?" he asked?

"No, we're neighbors. She's been away a long time and we're worried about her house and her dogs. We don't know what to do. Things need to be taken care of and we aren't sure how to help."

"Why don't you make an appointment with one of our administrators? There may be some informal ways you could help Susan and us, as we try to plan for her future, and there may be some legal proceedings that you could be made aware of."

The three of them sat down with one of the official administrators a few days later.

"I can't go into detail about Susan's situation," he told them. "However, it is quite unusual for such a young person to have no known relatives, and little evidence of caring friendships. What information we do have about her has been provided by her broker. Our staff has decided that it would be appropriate to convey some basic information to you as her neighbors. One, Susan will be in rehabilitation for quite some time. Because of her age and the type of strokes she has had, it is hopeful that she will regain her ability to walk and talk over time, as she participates in intensive therapy. Two, Susan's broker has informed us that Susan has the financial resources and insurance to cover all of her expenses. However, due to her inability to make informed decisions at this point, the court has assigned a guardian/conservator to her case to make appropriate health care decisions for her and to assist with managing her finances. This is the person you will need to contact with your questions and concerns."

"What about her dogs?"

"What?"

"She has six dogs. The neighbors have been taking care of them."

"You can discuss this with her guardian, but I'm sure it would be within your purview to relinquish them if they are a burden to you. They aren't your responsibility."

"Wow," was the only word any of the three of them spoke.

They left his office. "I'm not relinquishing those dogs just because it's within my *purview* to do so!" Sonia swore. The other two just solemnly shook their heads. "What a mess," Wendy said. Margaret nodded.

As they were leaving, they stopped to say "hello" to Susan. The three of them felt she was in a dreadful position. Without thinking, Sonia asked her, "Susan, would you like to see one of your dogs? We could sneak it in!"

Susan looked directly at Sonia. All of them agreed later that her expression had changed, though from what to what was hard to say.

"We'll be back!" Sonia promised.

And they were.

Lassie fit easily into Margaret's generous leather purse, and seemed charmed to be going on an adventure. They walked into the rehab center and found Susan sitting by the window again. They asked the staff it would be OK to visit with Susan in her room. It was, and they wheeled her down there. Margaret's bag was making noises and generating quite a bit of movement. They got to her room, shut the door, and sat on the bed across from Susan.

"Susan! We brought you a visitor!"

Margaret set her purse on the floor, and Lassie jumped out. She was so excited she just wiggled all over the place, barking happy little barks. Sonia picked her up and put her on Susan's lap. Lassie squirmed around and then put her paws on Susan's shoulders and began to wash her face and wash her face and wash her face. Happy dog! And, quite possibly, happy Susan. Hard to tell if the moisture on her cheeks was tears or dog spit.

For the next several weeks, Sonia, Wendy or Margaret would visit Susan with one of the dogs, until all six had eventually been carried to Susan's lap in Margaret's handbag. Their visits were clearly positive for Susan. She began to react to Margaret's bag as soon as she saw it, and attempted to wheel her chair in the direction of her room. As the summer wore on, the staff caught on to the doggie bag trick and gave permission for the dogs to visit officially. They could now prance in on leashes, and quickly became staff and patient favorites.

Margaret, Sonia and Wendy met with Susan's guardian/conservator, Wilma, who seemed relieved to know that someone, somewhere had met her client. She listened to their story of the events that had unfolded, and the neighbors' rescue of Susan's six dogs. She quickly approved some financial reimbursement out of Susan's account for the dogs' care and gave these neighbors permission and funding to have Susan's house painted. Sonia gave Wilma the box of mail. Wilma said she was now having the mail forwarded to her office. Wilma had been to Susan's house, taken note of the cars, original artwork, library, high-end stereo system, grand piano, etc. She had been astounded to find out that the house had no security system, and told them she was having one installed. She said she appreciated what the neighbors were doing to take care of Susan's dogs and yard, and asked them to get in touch with her at any time if something seemed amiss or if they had questions. As their meeting came to a close, Wilma said, "Susan's broker has told me that she is an accomplished pianist. Did you know that?" The three of them were stunned. "He told me that Susan had played for him several times over the years, and that she played with great emotion. He said that her little dogs would gather under the piano and lie down to listen. When she finished a piece, they would whine at her until she played something else. They especially liked Leybach's 5th Nocturne. Can you believe it?"

Wendy, Sonia and Margaret stumbled outside. They had formed their opinion of Susan from brief, negative interactions and from observing a house in need of paint and a yard that was accumulating trash. That Susan could have another side to her, especially one that involved playing classical music for her dogs, was beyond their comprehension. Sonia said, "Well, I guess it's true that *you can't judge a book by its cover.*" Wendy just groaned.

Susan began to talk, not well, but earnestly. Her first attempts came as greetings to her dogs, and she named them as they jumped in her lap. The neighbors couldn't understand the names as Susan spoke them, and continued to call them by their temporary names. As time went by, her communications sounded more like orders than conversation, but she was clearly improving. They liked her better when she couldn't talk, but listened patiently as she attempted to communicate with them. There was some staff talk about having her move home with a full-time caregiver at some point in the future. In the meantime, Sonia thought Susan might enjoy listening to some piano music, and took her a CD player and some CDs on one of her visits. She thought Lassie might enjoy listening to some piano music as well, to remind her of home and Susan. So, she bought Lassie her own CD player. She couldn't find a recording of the Fifth Nocturne, so went with a CD of Chopin's greatest hits. Results were mixed.

Sonia and Mark decided to plant a ginkgo tree in Susan's front yard. It would serve as a reminder that someone lived there, or did, and might again. It was the neighborhood's sixth ginkgo tree. They liked the way the ginkgo grove was shaping up along their street, giving a boost to the character of the neighborhood and pulling it together in some way. Then, they got the idea that maybe Stan and Mike might want to plant one when they ran the marathon in their 50th state. That way, the tree could be a celebration tree, or an achievement tree in addition to its role as a remembrance tree. In fact, maybe more neighbors would participate if they didn't think they had to have a stroke or move away or die to have their own ginkgo tree. Something to think about.

Mark knocked on Tom's door. When Tom opened it, Mark said, "Tom, we're going to be painting Susan's house this weekend. We could sure use your help."

Margaret was driving along a rural road trying to piece together the dream she had had that morning, just before waking up. She suddenly noticed the haystacks rolled up and dotting the hillsides on either side of the road. She was jolted into the present. Was it fall? What had happened to summer? Why was she wearing a jacket? Did her shoes match?

Jimmy Bittlemeier

Jimmy Bittlemeier could have been invisible as the 5th child in a set of six little Bittlemeier children. He wasn't the oldest. He wasn't exotic like his Chinese sister. He wasn't adopted, didn't have a heart condition, and hadn't died young. He wasn't a twin. He wasn't the only remaining girl, and he wasn't the baby of the family. He was stuck in the line-up well past the middle, and could have gotten very little attention as #5 if it hadn't been for the circumstances surrounding his birth. He grew up knowing about his near-birth in a Porta-Potty during the great "Hands across America" event that took place the day he was born. He also understood, without being told, that something special was expected of him after all his parents had gone through that day in their efforts to connect him to the world. The way he saw it, he had two options for a career that would please his parents: he could build on the "hands" theme and become a hand surgeon, or he could become President of the United States like his namesake, Jimmy Carter. Both were daunting thoughts.

On days that he didn't care about pleasing his parents, he loved to play with the idea of a career built around his signature birth event. What if he went into waste management? That would fit and would garner some attention. He could become a manicurist, a palm reader, a handball champion, a sign language interpreter, a "handyman." He wondered what his parents would think if he, like his namesake, became a peanut farmer. He did like peanut butter awfully well.

Jimmy's career choice was influenced, and ultimately decided by the unfortunate circumstance of having a friend accidentally amputate his left hand with an electric saw in shop class in high school. Jimmy was there. He saw it happen. In fact, the hand had flown off and landed right at Jimmy's feet. He had the presence of mind to react quickly. He picked it up, wrapped it in his shirt and raced with it to the school cafeteria where he put it in the salad bar and covered it with ice. His instructor, who still had his job for a few brief hours, fainted. Another student grabbed the hand-less arm and squeezed it shut until the ambulance arrived. The hand was retrieved from the salad bar and was miraculously reattached. It never functioned at 100% but it looked pretty good. "Wow," was all Jimmy could say.

Hand surgeon it was.

Jim graduated from high school with good grades, was accepted at a state university, graduated, applied for and was accepted into medical school, and completed a five-year residency in orthopedic surgery. After that, he enrolled in a one-year fellowship focused on trauma surgery of the hand and wrist. At the age of 31, Dr. Bittlemeier was a board-certified hand surgeon, preparing to join a surgical practice. He wondered if peanut farming would have been any easier. He also wondered if taking shop in high school as an elective could have led to a less stressful career choice, if it hadn't been for that hand.

In the end, Jim had a career his parents could be proud of. He could have gotten some of the attention he deserved, if not for the fact that his baby brother Del showed up with the first Bittlemeier grandchild just as Jim was launching his career, forcing him back into sibling obscurity.

Iris Mahoney

Where in the world was Wendy's daughter? Did she exist outside of Wendy's dreams of her? Was she nearby? Was her name *Grace*, as Wendy has imagined it? Could they nearly have met over Thompson's seedless grapes? Was she an artist? Was she happy? Details are sketchy, but let's just say that, while Wendy's necklace and gold footprint are probably lost forever, Wendy's daughter isn't lost. She is just far, far away, and it isn't likely that Wendy will meet her, especially since she isn't really looking for her. Her name isn't Grace, it's Iris, and she has bloomed where she was planted.

There is a strip mall on the edge of the town of Hasseltine, New Jersey. This strip mall is 1,324 driving miles from the end of Wendy's driveway. It has all of the amenities Americans have grown to expect in edge-of-town strip malls: a liquor store, a used clothing store with collection bins out front, a coffee bar, a manicure and tanning salon, a gas station that carries cigarettes every day and hot donuts on Sunday, a Chinese take-out, and, at the very end, a tattoo parlor with a red neon sign that says OPEN, most of the time. The strip mall seems to be well-placed in terms of attracting passersby, and even though the various businesses change from time to time, there are never empty storefronts.

Iris Mahoney is one of two tattoo artists who work at the Tit for Tat. She has been at this business since it opened, and had worked previously at several other tattoo parlors. She is good at what she does, and has many repeat customers. She herself is covered in tattoos. Her neck and back comprise one whole canvas, mostly green and blue, with a female spirit of some sort emerging in swirls from the base of her spine. She has a variety of butterflies on her legs and a rainbow just over her belly button. One arm is covered in roses. The other is inscribed with a passage from Walt Whitman's *Leaves of Grass*: "Missing me one place, search another . . . I stop somewhere, waiting for you." There are two equally elaborate hearts on the left side of her chest. Each heart contains the word "Mom." Iris thinks one day she will follow the clues she has assembled that could lead to her birth mother. Or, she won't. She does dream about this person and calls her Serena. She thinks Serena would like to meet her son, Beau, someday. Maybe tomorrow. Or next month. Or next year. Or not.

"If you had a lot of money and decided you wanted to use some of it to build a subdivision, what would you call it?"

Reuben was driving the car and glanced at Wendy sideways, trying to ascertain how seriously to take her question.

"Uh, I don't know. What do you mean?"

"I'm just thinking about names and wondering if the name of a place determines the character of the people who live there, or if it's the other way around. What would be a good name, do you think?"

"Well, I know some names I wouldn't use, like Cowboy Ridge or Country Acres or Heavenly Heights."

She laughed. "Yes, definitely not Heavenly Heights, especially if weather vanes are required. But what kind of name would make you happy to live there?"

"I hadn't really thought about it. I'm happy where we are. I like our life. The name isn't important."

"How 'bout Ginkgo Glen?"

"Ginkgo Glen? Living in a subdivision called Ginkgo Glen would make you happier?"

"Not happier. Just happy."

"Are you thinking of that name since so many of us now have ginkgo trees?"

"I guess."

"Well, I suppose we could refer to it that way, but I doubt that it would work for an actual name."

"Why not?"

"Well, for one thing, we live on a hill. A glen is a valley."

"I know, but Ginkgo Hill isn't as fun to say. Besides, it's been called Heavenly Heights for all these years and you can't say that's accurate."

Reuben laughed. They drove in silence for a while.

"What would a place called Ginkgo Glen be like?" Reuben said, as they approached their home.

"Oh, all the houses would have ginkgo trees in the front yards just like in our neighborhood, and in the fall, all the leaves would turn yellow at exactly the same time and then fall off at exactly the same time. The roofs would be yellow, the porches would be yellow, the yards would be yellow and when the people came outside, they'd be yellow too."

"I'm not fond of yellow."

"I know."

They did have a block party. It happened on a warm Saturday afternoon in the fall. Wendy hoped that the ginkgo trees would drop their leaves that very day. It hadn't happened yet, but the day was still young. Neighbors up and down the street had been invited with notices placed in their mailboxes, and a good percentage of the subdivision was in attendance.

The center of festivities was Reuben and Wendy's driveway, and Reuben was setting up card tables for food. "Hey, look!" Reuben shouted to Wendy as people converged on their driveway. "It's a People Parade!"

"So it is!" she shouted back happily, as she maneuvered down their front steps with a tray of sandwiches.

They had gotten a permit to block off their street, so there was plenty of room to sit or mingle without having to worry about traffic. While Reuben set up tables, others deposited lawn chairs here and there and added their contributions to the community potluck. In addition to Wendy's sandwiches, there was a variety of salads and chips and drinks and cookies and one very yummy-looking chocolate cake. Mark brought his ladder over and helped Wendy install her new yellow neon gingko leaf in the space over the garage. Its glow was mesmerizing, and, when it got dark, would be seen for blocks. There were murmurs about putting one on some of the other houses. Reuben didn't object, but quietly hoped that this, too, would pass.

All the dogs were there. Porky and Archie came with their new caretakers, Stan and Mike. Dolly had been renamed "Ralph" for reasons that should have been obvious, and had been relocated to Tom's house. Reuben and Wendy were keeping Queen Mary; she was adapting to life with two cats. Baby was trying out life at Margaret's house; she especially liked the shoe room. Lassie, of course, was staying with Sonia and Mark. Her puppies were due any day. There were several candidates for their daddy. The commuters came. As it turned out, they both had names and daily destinations. Harley worked as a bodyguard for a local celebrity in the state capital. Ginger spent each day with her aging mother at a nursing home in Kansas City. Ginger had noticed the proliferation of ginkgo trees and had heard the story that they were planted as remembrance trees. She quietly thought that a new ginkgo tree would probably need to be planted for her mother by the time spring rolled around again, and that thought made her feel a bit better about what was to come.

The computer geeks had not responded to the block party notices, so everyone was surprised when they, too, showed up. An even bigger surprise was the arrival of Susan, looking pale and weak, wheeled down the ramp of a special transport van. She lit up when she saw all of her dogs, and many of them spent time on and off her lap during the short time she was able to stay. Lassie had difficulty jumping up onto Susan's lap, and there was some shrieking and possibly some cursing when Susan realized why. Once she recovered from the shock, she firmly reminded everyone that the dogs belonged to her. ALL of the dogs. Current and future. She swore that she would be back some day and expected the dogs to be clean and free of fleas. She looked over toward her house and managed to let everyone know that she didn't like the color that her house had been painted, even though it was just a fresh coat of the same color it had been. She thought her grass had been mowed too short, and what was that ugly tree doing in her yard anyway? Before she left, she asked Sonia, if she wouldn't mind, if she'd give the house a good cleaning. "Thank you" didn't seem to be in her vocabulary. In spite of her demeanor, everyone made a point of introducing themselves to her, and some even gave her hugs, causing her to curse again (but more softly), thereby giving her more opportunities to practice her speaking.

Reuben made a map of their neighborhood. He titled it, "The People Parade of Ginkgo Glen." Each house up and down the block was represented by a rectangle. Those who wanted to participate could put their names, addresses and phone numbers inside their rectangles when the map was passed around. The Computer Geeks took the information, left briefly to scan it into a computer and returned with printed copies to give to everyone so they'd know their neighbors' names and how to contact each other. There was no immediate plan to distribute these maps to tourists.

Bruce came with Margaret. Sonia and Mark brought their son Del, his wife and baby, who were visiting from St. Louis. Sonia came wearing a stylish jacket made of a canvas material decorated with dachshunds, and carrying a plastic grocery bag that may have held a few beanbags.

Tom brought a tuna casserole.

The End

IN OTHER'S WORDS
by
Sonia Bittlemeier

for

M Theresa Bittlemeier (Emmie)
our first daughter, b. 1978

Mahatma Gandhi Bittlemeier (Matt)
our first son, b. 1981

Martin Luther King Bittlemeier (Marty)
our second son, b. 1981

Bertha von Suttner Bittlemeier (Bertie)
our second daughter, b. 1984

James Earl Carter Bittlemeier (Jimmy)
our third son, b. 1986

Nelson Mandela Bittlemeier (Del)
our surprise fourth son, b. 1993

~

Malala Yousefzai Bittlemeier, (Molly), our first
granddaughter, b. 2017

~

Blessed are the peacemakers.
Remember your names. Act accordingly.

I have long been afflicted with the frequent, and often irritating, use of clichés, quotations and song lyrics in the place of original conversation and thought. With tongue firmly in cheek, I will take this bull by its horns and attempt to use it to my advantage to convey something of my life in a format that those of you who know me, will recognize. I have thought of doing this many times over the last several years, but I've kept it on the back burner. I'm not getting any younger, and right now I'm on a roll. The way I see it, there's no time like the present, and it's better late than never. After all, a journey of a thousand miles, starts with a single step. The results may be a bit rough around the edges, but who knows, maybe I'll knock it out of the park. At least I can run it up the flagpole and see who salutes.

I just have a few things I want to say. I have loved being your mother, and will love being Molly's grandmother, and grandmother to others who may follow. But, I haven't just held you inside me next to my heart, rocked you, taken care of you when you were sick, watched your first steps and worried as you learned to ride a bike. I haven't just made you eat your vegetables, washed dishes and clothes and driven you to school and sports events, put your drawings on the refrigerator or worried as you began to date or went off to college. What I'm trying to say is that I have had roles other than that of a mother: child, sibling, student, girlfriend, wife, lover, colleague, teacher, friend, neighbor and dog collector, to name a few. I know you are cringing to think of me as girlfriend or lover, but get used to it. You weren't born yesterday.

I am a person. I was a person before you came into my life, tried to be a person while you were all at home (without much success), and am learning to be a person again now that you are all people in your own right. You could say I'm back in the saddle again.

I have a name. Sonia.

I was not a beautiful baby or a beautiful child, and have never been considered a beautiful woman. Instead, I think of myself, as Lucile Clifton writes, *plain as bread, round as a cake, an ordinary woman.* I don't feel that I had a happy childhood. I identify with the line in a Langston Hughes poem, *life for me ain't been no crystal stair.* I had two brothers who fought all the time and parents who divorced. But then, I always heard that what doesn't kill you, makes you stronger. I believe this has been true in my life. My ongoing wish has been . . . can't we all just get along? In my youth, I was attracted to the peace movement that defined that era. I loved singing, *Let there be peace on earth, and let it begin with me,* and tried in all kinds of circumstances to let peace begin with me. I greatly admire those who choose non-violent resistance in the face of seemingly overwhelming odds. That moral stance has been a defining objective for me throughout my life.

When I was growing up, we had very little money and had to tighten our belts constantly. I held several jobs, worked hard, and had to scrape to get through college, but I did. Somehow the children's story about Thomas and the little blue engine helped me form a positive attitude: *I think I can, I think I can, I think I can.* I kept my nose to the grindstone and somehow, even when I was at the end of my rope, was always able to pull rabbits out of a hat.

Everything changed for the better when I met Mark. I fell head over heels for him. I suppose meeting him was just the luck of the draw. But, because of him, I was finally able to look at the world through rose-colored glasses. There aren't enough love songs to pay him tribute. We made a good team, and had a good time, too. I've always thought of this as our song: *Let it be a dance we do, may I have this dance with you, through the good times and the bad times, too, let it be a dance.* Six children and many years later, I can say he's still the one, the pot of gold at the end of the rainbow.

Parenting has been baptism by fire. We didn't know what we were doing as we were going through it, and we still don't. We just flew by the seat of our pants. It seems there was always a bun or two in the oven, and I was tickled pink by this. I loved the whole kit and caboodle of you and thought the more the merrier. You all grew like weeds and gave us a laugh a minute. Becoming a mother the first time, took a long time, and then Emmie was with us . . . *soft as little pigeon* eggs . . . and then she was snatched away. It is said that only the good die young, but that didn't make it any easier. I wish she had been able to know the rest of you. What a family we had! How did we ever survive? If . . . *A little chaos is good for the soul . . .* at least our souls were in good shape. It seemed like an entire era of five little monkeys jumpin' on the bed. And then, the monkeys were gone.

Whenever I have felt smug about any of you, who you are or what you have done, Kahlil Gibran's lines run through my head: *Your children are not your children, they are the sons and daughters of life's longing for itself.* This works to temper my pride and boastfulness when you accomplish something magnificent, and gets me off the hook when you go off on the wrong track.

I loved being a mother, but I loved being a teacher, too. Having a career was the icing on the cake. I felt it was important to not just teach facts, but to allow kindness to have space in my classroom and to be a role model. This old Edgar Guest poem was always at the back of my mind:

The lectures you deliver may be very wise and true,
But I'd rather get my lesson by observing what you do.
For I may misunderstand you and the high advice you give,
But there's no misunderstanding how you act and
    how you live . . .

I have had wonderful friends and colleagues. We've shared great laughs and good deeds and talked it all out. Now, I've grown older. I look in the mirror and think, gee, whiz. Who is that? Sometimes, ya just gotta laugh. If I said that once, I said it a thousand times.

Now, I'm an oldie but goodie. The clock is ticking. Have I accomplished anything? The jury is still out. I think about death and life after death. Like most people, I do wonder what it's all about, and if anybody is out there. I have no answers, and no advice to pass along.

In closing, I acknowledge with gratitude that I have had a good life. I apologize for not being original, but what you see is what you get. I aspire in the time I have left to be the person my dog thinks I am.

I have now written this document. While writing it hasn't been a piece of cake, it is now signed, sealed and delivered. Someday, you'll thank me for it. With that, to make a long story short, I rest my case.

I did it! I wrote it!
But, then,
I thought I could, I thought I could, I thought I could!

(Last but not least, a special note to my friend Wendy, who rescued me when it was raining cats and dogs. Well, mostly dogs. Ok, just dogs. Thank you for your help with our little dachshund friends. What an adventure! It was fun. Well, mostly. And, thank you for listening as I explored this crazy writing idea. Because you questioned the existence of fruit clichés, I will close with these, just for you: As our neighborhood has come together, we have found that life can be just a bowl of cherries. And, now that my "autobiography" has been written, everything is peaches and cream!)

Have a nice day!

THE NOBEL PEACE PRIZE

The Nobel Peace Prize was established as one of five beneficiaries in the will of Alfred Nobel, a Swedish chemist (1833 – 1896). The prize has been given out annually since 1901. The qualification for receiving the award was outlined in the will as, "the person who shall have done the most or best work for fraternity between nations, the abolition or reduction of standing armies and for the holding and promotion of peace congresses" (www.nobelprize.org).

MAHATMA GANDHI, (1869 -1948), of India, was nominated for the Nobel Peace Prize five times (1937, 1938, 1939, 1947 and 1948), but it was never awarded to him. He is described on the Nobel Peace Prize website as "the strongest symbol for non-violence in the 20th century." He led non-violent campaigns against British authority, leading eventually to India's independence from Britain, and advocated for the unification of Hindus, Muslims and Christians.

MARTIN LUTHER KING, JR., (1929-1968), of the United States, was a prominent American leader in the civil rights movement. He was awarded the Nobel Peace Prize in 1964 for his work toward achieving social justice for all.

BARONESS BERTHA VON SUTTNER, (1843 – 1914), of Austria, was the first woman to be awarded the Nobel Peace Prize. It is said that it was her friendship with Alfred Nobel that led to the establishment of the prize. She was an author and peace activist, and received the Nobel Peace Prize in 1905.

JAMES EARL CARTER, (1924 -   ), 39th president of the United States (1977 - 1981), was awarded the Nobel Peace Prize in 2002 for decades of untiring effort to find peaceful solutions to international conflict.

NELSON MANDELA, (1918-2013), one of South Africa's first black lawyers, was awarded the Nobel Peace Prize in 1993 for his work toward the dismantling of the apartheid regime, laying the foundation for a new, democratic South Africa. He was arrested for his activism, incarcerated from 1964 to 1990, and was considered the world's most famous political prisoner. After his release, he was elected president of South Africa.

MALALA YOUSAFZAI, (1997 -   ), of Pakistan, was awarded the Nobel Peace Prize in 2014 for her work as an activist for female education and human rights. She is the youngest recipient to date.

(All notes taken from: www.nobelprize.org, March 4, 2018)

The Consent

Late in November, on a single night
Not even near to freezing, the ginkgo trees
That stand along the walk drop all their leaves
In one consent, and neither to rain nor to wind
But as though to time alone: the golden and green
Leaves litter the lawn today, that yesterday
Had spread aloft their fluttering fans of light.

What signal from the stars? What senses took it in?
What in those wooden motives so decided
To strike their leaves, to down their leaves,
Rebellion or surrender? and if this
Can happen thus, what race shall be exempt?
What use to learn the lessons taught by time,
If a star at any time may tell us: Now.

~Howard Nemerov
(1920-1991)

Poet Laureate of the United States 1963-64, and 1988-90
Winner of the Pulitzer Prize for poetry, 1978

AUTHOR'S NOTE

I first paid attention to the ginkgo when I saw photographs and scans of the leaves taken by Bill Bowerman, a member of a photography club I had been attending. I loved the shape of the leaves and the purity of their yellowness, made even more beautiful by the clarity of this artist's photography.

We have four ginkgo trees that grow between the street and sidewalk just down the hill from our house. For about 360 days a year, these trees are almost invisible. When their leaves turn yellow in the fall, seemingly all at the same time, they are glorious. I happened to be walking by those four trees some years ago, and only noticed them at all because there were four of them and they were uniformly yellow. I couldn't wait to photograph them. But I did wait, until the next day. When I returned that next day with my camera, I was shocked to see that every leaf had fallen since the day before. How could this be?

I was terribly disappointed, and vowed that I would pay better attention the following year. That second year, I made sure my daily walks included a pass by those ginkgo trees so that I could take note of any changes as soon as they occurred. I made sure to carry my camera with me. The leaves never did turn yellow that year, so I was caught by surprise when one day they were green on the tree, and the next day, they were green on the ground.

It wasn't until I read Nemerov's eloquent poem that I realized that this ginkgo phenomenon that I had observed was wider than my own perception of it. Their sudden release of leaves, without obvious rhyme or reason, was just what ginkgo trees did. I found this mystery to be enchanting and fell in love with ginkgoes. Like Wendy, I could be happy living in a Ginkgo Glen.

I am fortunate that there is a Ginkgo Glen within driving distance of my home in Lawrence, Kansas. I discovered recently that the back lawn of the Nelson-Atkins Museum of Art in Kansas City has an abundance of these trees. In five levels leading down the hillside from the back steps of the museum, there are 16 trees growing in each of four of the levels, and 15 trees growing in the other level (with the 16th spot in that level given over to a Rodin sculpture), for a total of 79.

The ginkgo tree is native to China. It is thought to be the earth's oldest living organism. Its seeds have been found in fossils, 270 million years old. Some living trees are thought to be 1,500 years old. In addition to the plantings at the Nelson, there is an entire ginkgo grove at Washington University in St. Louis, where one can observe these lovely life forms from the windows of the Nemerov Library.

ACKNOWLEDGMENTS

Many thanks to Ann James, who runs, and who provided me with first-hand information about marathon running; to Bob Nitcher, who helped me understand the art and science of neon; to Frank Taff for giving Susan Cochran a broker; to Jill Glinka, OTR, for advice on weighted vests; to Susan Henderson for infusing me with enthusiasm for *Jayhawks on Parade*; to Tracy Million Simmons for rescuing the book's shape and presentation; and to my friend Kathy Koplik for her keen editing eye and continuing support.

About the Cover . . .

Janet Rose Bailey is a watercolor artist, now based in Savannah Georgia. I met her many years ago in Topeka, Kansas, and have always loved her work as an artist. At one of her early exhibits, I was able to acquire a beautiful landscape that she had painted *en plein air* from a hillside looking to the south over Topeka from Menninger Hill. Janet specializes in bright colors, applied in translucent layers. She says she is "inspired by nature and the galaxy, with paintings that are energetic and vibrantly hued." She was the first person who came to my mind as I contemplated art work for the cover of this book. Her delicate rendering of ginkgo leaves superimposed on a brilliant yellow background hints at the moment that all will be swept away with the wind. To me, this perfectly expresses the mystery of the ginkgo, and can be thought of as a metaphor for our fragile, often tentative connections with each other as we make our way through life.

RESOURCES

American Art Parades. Karlynn Keyes and Rod Barker. The Trail of Painted Ponies, Inc., Carefree, AZ, 2007. This is a large picture book showing some of the creations exhibited in over 200 art parades all across America.

Cows on Parade in Chicago.
Kreuzlingen, Switzerland: Neptun Verlagsauslieferung, 1999. This book shows photographs of most of the 200 cows that were on display in the first cow parade in America.

Hands across America, the Official Record Book. New York: Pocket Books, a division of Simon & Schuster, Inc., 1986. This book tell the story of how the event developed, how the route was determined, who participated and who benefited from it.

Jayhawks on Parade. Lawrence, Kansas: The Kansas Alumni Association, 2003. This book has a history of the University of Kansas mascot, the Jayhawk. There are photographs of the 30 Jayhawks on Parade in 2003, a map of where each Jayhawk was located, and the story of how the parade developed.

Nemerov, Howard. "The Consent." *Western Approaches*. Chicago: University of Chicago Press, 1975.

Ribbat, Christoph. *Flickering Light, a History of Neon.* London: Reaktion Books Ltd., 2011.

Smallman, Etan. "Making dazzling art from Neon Lights." *The Guardian* (January 10, 2015): http://www.theguardian.com/lifeandstyle/2015/jan/10/make-dazzling-art-neon-lights.

SONG LYRICS

LITERARY QUOTATIONS

135   I think I can, I think I can, I think I can . . . from *The Little Engine that Could*; best known incarnation written by Watty Piper, 1930.

136   Soft as little pigeon-eggs. . . from the poem, "Little Girl Be Careful What You Say," in the poetry book *Wind Song*, by Carl Sandburg. New York: Harcourt, Brace & World, 1960.

136   Your children are not your children . . . from "On Children," in *The Prophet*, by Lebanese poet and artist Kahlil Gibran, 1973.

136   Perfection is death; life is better than order; a little chaos is good for the soul . . . Mira, in *Women's Room*, by Marilyn French. New York: Summit Books, 1977.

137   The lectures you deliver may be very wise and true . . . from the poem, "Sermons We See," in the book, *The Light of Faith*, by Edgar Guest; published by Reilly and Lee Co., 1926.

138   I thought I could, I thought I could, I thought I could . . . from *The Little Engine that Could*; best known incarnation by Watty Piper, 1930.

POPULAR SAYINGS

59   *What's the matter, Lassie? Is Timmy in the well?* . . . A catchphrase that evolved from the television series, Lassie" (1954-1973), referring to the many situations in which the little boy Timmy's welfare was in jeopardy; Timmy never did actually fall into a well and the phrase was never spoken on the series.

71   *Houston, we have a problem* . . . a version of this statement is attributed to the crew of Apollo 13 (1970) and memorialized in the film "Apollo 13" with Tom Hanks.

135   *Can't we all just get along?* . . . A version of this question is attributed to Rodney King, Los Angeles (1992).

137   *Lord, help me to be the person my dog thinks I am* . . . a popular bumper sticker

CLICHÉS, IDIOMS AND FIGURES OF SPEECH

Definitions for the following seem obvious. Specific information about each one can be found easily online, especially using the-freedictionary.com, yahoo.answers.com, and/or Wikipedia.com.

47	There's a fool born every minute
48	a few cards short of a full deck . . .
48	a few bricks short of a load . . .
49	Her light's on, but no one's home
61	Something is rotten in Denmark

A version of the phrase *Something seems rotten in the state of Denmark,* from Act 1, Scene 4 of *Hamlet,* by William Shakespeare. The phrase is often used to imply that something is wrong with the current situation.

122	You can't judge a book by its cover
133	tongue in cheek
134	take the bull by its horns
134	put it on the back burner
134	not getting any younger
134	on a roll
134	no time like the present
134	better late than never
134	journey of 1,000 miles begins with a single step
134	rough around the edges
134	knock it out of the park
134	run it up the flagpole
134	wasn't born yesterday
135	back in the saddle
135	what doesn't kill you makes you stronger
135	tighten belts
135	nose to the grindstone
135	end of my rope
135	pull a rabbit out of a hat
135	fall head over heels
136	luck of the draw
136	rose-colored glasses
136	pot of gold at the end of the rainbow